Zoe Taylor's Story

Confessions of a Cigarette Addict

N. L. BRISSON

ISBN:0692801588
ISBN-13:9780692801581

This is a work of fiction in the form of a memoir. Any resemblance to real people is a testament to my love for the people in my life. I have given only brief vignettes that hardly suffice to present to you a three-dimensional view of anyone I know. Some of these events may have actually happened, or not. Some of these people may have been present for some of these events, some not so much. If you think you recognize someone, it is not really them. But addiction is real and addicted people often do bad or stupid stuff to feed their addiction. Cigarette addiction seems tame compared to some forms of addiction, but it can kill you. Cocaine and heroin were available in the 60's and have been for centuries. Opioids are new and they may be the most life-destroying chemicals we have ever experienced. If you have an addiction, even to cigarettes, get help or you may derail your life or even die too soon.

Dedicated to all the Taylors,

real or fictional

Confessions of a Cigarette Addict

Introduction

Hello, Zoe Taylor here. The things that I did and the things that happened to me can only be traced to my cigarette addiction. Perhaps there were tiny seeds and character flaws from my childhood that made me prone to my addiction, or maybe it can be traced to a chemical imbalance, fluctuating serotonin levels. Maybe it was a little glitch in my DNA, dormant until that first inhalation of hazy, gray smoke. You can judge for yourself.

But there is no doubt in my mind that the weaknesses in my character steeped in smoke, tar, CO_2, and nicotine led to events through which I degraded myself and eventually rewrote my future.

This is not a story about how I overcame cancer, although that story may be waiting for me still down the line. This is story that proves that the effects of our actions can be completely unpredictable; that explores the nature of addiction and the way it self-destructs our best instincts.

Chapter 1

The Taylors

The Taylor family started out in a city apartment in a medium-sized city in central New York, right at the end of World War II. We played air raid in our front yard. When the city held tests of the air raid sirens, we had to crouch down next to the cellar wall. Then we had to check up over us to make sure there were no windows above us. If there were, we had to scuttle along to a new window-free position and wait for the all clear. This was before the US dropped the first atomic bomb. This was in anticipation of just your regular old everyday average bomb like the ones that made life an insecure misery in London during the war.

Sometimes we walked to the little grocery store on the corner, at first with Mom, later we were allowed to go by ourselves, since we didn't have to cross any streets. Most of the time, we just ran around making up games with the rest of the kids in the neighborhood or sat in the back driveway with Mom while she hung out the laundry.

Felicity, my older sister, was born first: pale, anemic, two months premature (she almost died, we often heard), delicate and pretty. Zoe, that's me, I was born second: chubby, full term and jealous as hell of my dainty "big" sister (second child syndrome much?). According to family lore, I followed Mom and Felicity as soon as I learned to crawl and bit their ankles whenever I got the chance. Soon after I was born came Tyler, the long-awaited son, blond and handsome, with curls all over his precious little head. Not even a year later we got Gertrude, (Gertie) also a chubby, but with a cherub-sunny face and perfect golden brown ringlets. By the time we got Robert, a devilish, blond crew cut little tough boy, we no longer fit in a two-bedroom apartment.

Dad, Hobart Taylor, found a house in the country, only about ten minutes from our old place in the city. Augusta, my mom was not happy that he picked it out all by himself, but was very happy to get the seven of us out of that crowded apartment.

By the way, as you can probably tell, we were poor. My dad had to leave school in the eighth grade to take care of his parents. Fortunately, he got some training in electrical matters. By the time we moved to Smithvale, he was working at GE and was in the electrician's union. Mom, with five small children, was not employed, in fact, I never remember her being away from us, except to have babies.

I was seven when we arrived in Smithvale and I don't remember much of that first year except a big old house with floral wallpapers, crackled white radiators everywhere you looked, and lots of grassy lawn. Already, by seven and eight, Felicity and I were often in charge of the younger kids. There were a lot of neighbor kids on our street. A few newer type subdivision houses were popping up here and there.

Mom's life changed little. She still spent hours rinsing diapers, soaking little outfits covered in spit up and later in dirt, and putting everything through the wringer washer in the basement. No wonder she loved to hang the clean, wet laundry on the line. It was a chance to be outside, even though she usually had at least two toddlers hanging on her skirts or pedal pushers. She put her hair up in pin curls after Dad left and tied a folded scarf around her head, and even like that we thought she was pretty.

Felicity and I knew how to heat bottles by then, how to test them on our wrists and hand them out to little snot-nosed Robert. Some days were just chaos, morning to night, although three of us were in school by then. Mom still had two at home and by the times we got back from school everyone would be ready to sit down in a little line in front of the TV to watch Howdie Doodie, with little cups of cereal to munch on. I just loved that Princess Summerfall, Winterspring.

The theory was that Mom would remove the scarf and pin curls from her hair shortly before Dad got home and primp herself up a little bit for him. At first this theory was put into practice religiously, but after a while the pin curls were often in place for several days at a time, hence the number of family photos that show our pretty young Mom with a bandana wrapped around her head. There is no doubt that her life was better in Smithvale than in the city. We could all be outside so much and Felicity and I could keep an eye on the tag-a-longs so Mom didn't have to be outside every time we were.

Winters were harder. All five of us had to be helped into snowsuits and boots and hats, and mittens and scarves. We were usually out about five minutes, then we were back, tracking melting snow everywhere and all needing to be undressed at once. And there were always the random bathroom emergencies when Mom had to shift into high gear and race to the bathroom with a child balance on a hip, tucked in under her left arm, booted feet flapping in the air, set down in front of the toilet and just the essential parts unwrapped. That she was usually successful in preventing an accident is a testament to her dislike of laundering those bulky snowsuits in mid-winter.

No new babies arrived for a couple of years which gave us all a little breather. On good days Mom would cut little sandwiches out of white bread with cookie cutters and stage little tea parties, and of course, there were tons of birthdays to celebrate with double layered frosted cakes and glowing candles and "Happy Birthday" and ice cream and presents. There was Easter and Christmas to break up the year and visits to our aunts and uncles who drank lots of beer and played the piano and sang "Nothing Could Be Finer Than to Be in Carolina" and "Show Me the Way to Go Home." Mom took off her bandana for all these occasions, except the one Easter when we all had the measles or the chicken pox and everyone went back to puking and crying as soon as we got over our Easter baskets.

Some of my aunts and uncles smoked, although Mom and Dad never did. Grampa Taylor smoked big old smelly cigars and our favorite, funny Aunt Mable smoked cigarettes and left an ashtray full of red-tipped butts each time she visited. In fact, I think all of my aunts and uncles smoked, but not like Aunt Mable. My handsome cousins were older than us but they didn't smoke yet.

After a couple of years of quiet on the baby front, just when we were all done with bottles and diaper changing, Mom and Dad started up again and produced three more girls, Emily, Rebecca and Morgan. I was nine when Emily was born, ten for Rebecca, and eleven when we got Morgan. It was getting embarrassing and the neighbors were aghast. But Morgan was the last one.

By then Mom was definitely swamped. If she kept up with the laundry, she forgot dinner and it was burned or so dry we couldn't eat it. Felicity and I learned to cook in self-defense so by eleven and twelve you could find us standing over the stove after school with a baby on our left hip stirring pots and checking ovens. We liked to cook.

We had outgrown out country home. Dad made do and carved new bedrooms out of attic space, freezing in winter, broiling in summer, but we were young and happy and had lots of friends and we didn't mind much. Life for Dad was a constant struggle involving day-old bread and gallons of milk and shoes, shoes, shoes. He didn't have to buy clothes very often because everyone we knew contributed boxes of castoffs which Mom and us older girls went through. The ironing piled up until Mom offered us a penny a piece and we learned to iron.

By the time I was five it was the 50's and by the time I was eleven, when the last baby was born, it was 1956. My sister and I were avid watchers of Syd Caesar, Milton Berle, and eventually The Hit Parade and Ed Sullivan, Father Knows Best, The Nelsons (Ozzie and Harriet) and I Love Lucy. We always had a TV. Dad was an electrician, after all, and everyone brought him broken sets to be fixed. He had lots of boxes of TV tubes in the basement with his oscilloscope and his voltmeter and he knew just which tubes to replace. No one smoked on TV in those days, except Dean Martin, who always had a cigarette hanging from his lips, maybe Lucy when she wanted to catch her hair on fire, and they did have these dancing cigarette boxes – box on top, underneath all legs, doing their Rockettes routine. Don't remember the brand, maybe Chesterfields.

By the time we were all in school I was about sixteen with two years of babysitting already under my belt. Mom would get up at 5 am to spread all the bread out on the kitchen counter to make sandwiches for us all for school. Dad was still working at GE, but Mom didn't drive, so when he got home from work he was in his taxi years. Mom volunteered him to drive for everything. My sister and I were both in a high school sorority, Alpha Mu Zeta. We made newspaper containers for cancer bandages and sang at old folks homes (as they were known then) and went to lots of meetings. Dad always had to pick up at least four other girls whose fathers were too busy to drive.

We went most summer Saturday afternoons to the Starlight Theater. It cost 35 cents at first, and later 50 cents. We saw every Doris Day movie and imagined ourselves into perfect designer apartments, cars and clothing with our reluctant, but lovesick gorgeous bachelor, who could not help giving up his glamorous single freedom, because he fell madly in love with one of us and now had no choice. I don't think Doris Day smoked in any of those movies but Rock sometimes did.

And, of course, we watched Elvis, but he never smoked. The tough hood guys who hung out at Mary's Pizza with their teased-out-hair girlfriends, they smoked. The bad boys wore their cigarette packs rolled up into their t-shirt sleeve. Annette Funicello and her crowd didn't smoke in the Beach Blanket movies. Everything was about s-e-x, and meeting the right guy. Even Tammy, the innocent poor country girl was always learning about s-e-x. And Gidget too! Maybe sex and cigarettes got mixed together for me.

Now we had, of course, pretended to smoke in our younger years. We loved nothing better than to take a quarter and go to the penny candy store. Candy cigarettes with their little red tips were one of the things we bought, along with the licorice replicas of 45-rpm records with the red candy center, and the waxy bottles with sweet syrup inside, and the Lik-a-Maids, and the watermelon slices.

We lived near an old air base so there were lots of abandoned barracks and obstacle courses, completely overgrown with meadow grasses. In my teen years the fire department burned an abandoned barracks every Thursday night, for practice, and to get rid of them. We would all run up and watch. It was better than fireworks. Mom would sometimes pack us picnic lunches in the summer and we would go into the meadows, find a clear spot and eat with our friends, maybe catch tadpoles or frogs. We would open the milkweed pods and scatter the silk and then cut down stalks with our mumbley-peg knives. After they dried out they were hollow and we would meet by the cellar stairs and try to smoke them. We also smoked cattails, holding the stems in our mouths, tapping off the ashes into the dirt around the cellar door.

Chapter 2

Why?

I guess I'm headed deep into the middle of the nature-nurture controversy here. Whence arose my addiction to cigarettes? Perhaps I can trace it to the insecurities of the second child syndrome. I've met a number of second children in my life and all seemed to have a strong thread of inferiority, self-image problems, running through their natures.

But in the 50's we didn't know from self-image.
Maybe sinister corporate strategies were at work, turning us into chimneys, as current information suggests. We didn't know from additives in the 50's either. Glamorous women in Hollywood films smoked. The Post World War II spirit of liberation for women, "the Rosie the Riveter" hype I guess you could call it, had all my adult female relatives (with the exception of my mom), and half our female neighbors puffing away.

Modern science, as far as we can tell, since it changes every five minutes, suggests that addiction is in the genes. You either have the marker for a particular addiction stamped into your DNA or you don't. As long as you never touch the object of you beastly predilection, you never push the biological button. Once you do turn the switch on though, it will be a bitch to turn it off.

You can sense that my childhood was a good one. Two responsible, upright parents; plenty to eat, drink, wear. My father, nicknamed Brain, pushed us to academic achievement and there were plenty of opportunities for childhood pursuits, role-playing, mischief, and plenty of companions. We made an ice rink in the winter, snow forts, pelted each other with snowballs, did homework, squabbled, and giggled. We dressed up every Halloween and marched around the neighborhood carrying huge sacks of candy. Our Christmases were shiny and tinselly enough for anyone. And our summers were spent outdoors with lemonade stands and baseball games and putting on plays and playing 'dolls' and 'house' and 'wedding' and 'war'. There were also endless games of "Hill Dill" and "Red Rover" and "Hide and Seek", tramps through meadows to catch fireflies, and being packed in the back of the station wagon in our jammies to go watch planes take off at the runway three blocks away.

It wasn't perfect, of course, it never is. Money was always a problem and we all knew it. Privacy was nonexistent, and disorder reigned indoors. Clothing, books, dishes, shoes, and toys covered every available surface. Space had to be cleared before any meal could be eaten or any homework done. Décor had no place in our lives. Our house always looked sloppy and ragged, but not dirty.

By the time high school rolled around we were starting to crave our own little corners. I made a bedroom in the back of the attic for a while, but after several fat lips from spider bites I had to abandon that plan. Once I moved out of Felicity 's and my room, it became impossible to move back in. I had a rollaway bed in the front foyer for a while.

Then there was the issue of boys. They all liked Felicity; none of them liked me. She was slender and blonde and pleasant, I was chubby and shy-eyed, giggly and full of energy, and had mousy brown hair. If I even looked at a boy he ran like hell in the opposite direction. This doesn't do a lot for your self-image. And she got all the best clothes that came into the house from the neighbors across the street who had three girls and an aunt who sewed beautifully. I forgot to mention church. My sisters and I spent a lot of time at church when we were in high school. We were in the junior choir and Bible study and Youth Fellowship. No one smoked there. These boys also liked Felicity better.

From early on I felt that my mother had gotten the shit end of the stick in the marital partnership between my Mom and my Dad. She was always with us kids for one thing. She never got to leave like my Dad. She never even got to sit down, unless it was to feed somebody. From five in the morning until ten or eleven at night she had more jobs to do than any one person could possibly accomplish. And they were all menial, repetitive jobs like doing dishes, changing kid's clothes about a hundred times a day and putting out the sprinkler to run through, then cleaning up the water from the floors when we all had to run to the bathroom, and pushing her hair, flying our of her pin curls, out of her hot, sticky face, and on, and on, and on. Her life was nothing like Doris Day.

I did not want to be her, although she didn't mind being her, most of the time. There was the day she just walked out, we didn't know where, desperate to get away. We knew she couldn't get far, because she didn't drive, and we no longer stood on the school bus corner believing the yellow bus would scoop us up anytime we stood there and take us to places unknown. So we just called around and tracked her down at the new K-Mart that had just opened across the highway, and we had her paged. She was not happy. I don't know how she did it but usually she was cheerful and comforting and kind. I still did not want to be her.

I decided I would never get married or have children because it was just a trap. You didn't get to do anything important, like go to plays, or eat out, or travel, or have a career. All you got to do was have your husband look down your blouse once in while or snap you with a dish towel and have more babies and cook more meals and have huge backyard cookouts, until your hair turned gray and eventually you died.

Now looking back, I can see that this was a rather jaundiced view of my mother's life, and an especially narrow view of what could be accomplished by a woman with perhaps fewer offspring and a higher standard of living. But I didn't live with those other mothers. I thought that what you see is what you get.

So I decided I wanted to go to college and be somebody, maybe an architect, or a writer, and live rich in NYC and have beautiful things around me all the time. I wanted to be Doris Day, but I wouldn't marry Rock Hudson because eventually, sure as hell, I'd just get to be a housewife, when I really wanted to be Emily Brontë, or Jane Austen, or even Emily Dickinson.

A friendly school dental hygienist decided to take our family on as a charity project and broaden our horizons. She took us one at a time to various events. Felicity missed out on this for some reason, but I got to go to the ballet, and out to lunch, the art museum, to a play, to the zoo. She was a very tall, very slender, very rigid lady with perfectly erect posture, and a very creepy, nerdy son. I always felt a little icky going off with them, but I loved the things we did. She, of course, did not smoke.

When I got into high school the staff had decided to try something new called tracking. They looked at your elementary grades (there were no middle schools or junior highs yet) and decided if you were 'basic', 'average', or 'above average'. If you looked like you fell into the above average category, they called you in individually and gave you an exhaustive IQ test involving blocks and spatial relationships, and even fact questions, everything timed. Felicity missed this by one year, but I was tested. I testing right on the borderline between average and honors, so it was decided that I could sign up for honors classes. This was a very lucky break for me.

Honors classes were excellent, especially honors English. I struggled with math. These students did not really misbehave. Even when someone made a joke, it was witty rather than thuggish. Someone made up jokes from trig equations (I wish I had copied them down, because to this day I cannot imagine how they did this) and wrote them on the board in "Bullwinkle's Corner".

I read and read and read. It was my privacy and my adventure. I could disappear into the world of a book and I would not even hear when someone called my name. I was on my way. Maybe I'd become a famous New York hostess and hold fabulous soirées in my Manhattan high rise.

Or maybe I'd hone the talents my sister and I had developed for designing outfits for our paper dolls and become the new Edith Head. She wasn't a pretty woman and look where she ended up. I graduated from high school in 1963. Everyone I knew was still living like the 50's would go on forever, with people just stockpiling more and more affluence, and appliances, and better cars in the garage, now that many families had two. I still wasn't smoking, had never touched a cigarette all through high school.

Chapter 3
Felicity

Felicity was 5'2", slender, with dirty blonde hair, blue eyes, and regular, but not beautiful, features. She was a true petite, with size 5 feet and skinny bones. She was quiet and responsible. I never remember her sobbing uncontrollably or having hissy fits, like some of us. She spent all of her time role-playing and preparing for a future right out of Future Homemakers of America. She had a best friend across the street named Carol and together they experimented with hair and makeup.

I tagged along with her often and she never complained in front of me, although I was boisterous and bossy and loud. We all had our baby dolls as I remember, which we held and fed and took for carriage rides. We didn't mistreat our babies. We were already experts on child care. I didn't want a baby doll. I wanted a Toni doll. Toni was the brand name of a home permanent kit. We had much practical experience of home permanents, since Mom was always slapping one onto our hair so she wouldn't have to fuss with our very straight, fine hair. To this day I can't recall the actual texture of Felicity's hair. Maybe she did have some natural curl. I surely didn't. Anyway the Toni doll came with a little permanent wave set, tiny curlers, and a wave solution so you could give your doll a perm. The directions said that when you ran out of permanent solution you could substitute sugar and water. Whenever you wanted you could wash the Toni doll's hair and it would straighten again, ready for the next perm. I was seven when I got my Toni doll and I permed the life right out of her.

There are also a number pictures of Felicity, Carol, and me playing cards on Carol's porch, or Sorry, or Parchesi. Carol had a beautiful bedroom too, which she didn't have to share with anybody. It was "decorated". We loved to spend time up there doing I don't remember what. I do remember that when Felicity and Carol were young teens they spent an afternoon practicing kissing techniques on each other, which I found very yucky at the time, but also fascinating. Things weren't always so easy for Felicity. Because she was the oldest she was sort of the guinea pig child. She had the most rules and because of her responsible nature, she took the rules pretty seriously. A lot of housework and child care duties fell to her. She was good in school and had lots of friends. Two boys were fighting over her by the time she was fourteen; a good-looking red-headed holy terror from the next block, Timothy Stanton, and an also handsome, slightly "hood"ish guy from across the main road. They hung around our house constantly, ate meals there, and strutted around each other cockily. Eventually my sister discarded both of them in favor of a slightly older guy, Jack Rhodes, from two blocks up.

When she graduated from high school with an award in Latin in 1962, she enrolled in the community college to train as a secretary. She lived at home while she went to college. Mom and Dad let her trade her bed in on a sofa bed and she could make her bedroom look like a little sitting room, and she could have boys up there. She was still with Jack Rhodes, but he was starting to balk. She wanted to get married, he didn't.

The "hoody" guy from across the highway reappeared. Dean Travis was his name. He was underfoot all the time again, this time trying to ingratiate himself with Mom and Dad and my brother, Tyler. He helped Dad spread stones in the driveway, fix cars, load newspapers to take to Spevak's for money, and with any number of small household repairs. In short he made himself indispensable and, although Felicity at first paid him no mind, he was like a force of nature. Eventually she stopped seeing the guys she was sort of dating and let him court her. Within three years of graduating high school she had finished community college, had her big wedding, decorated their new apartment, gone to work as an executive secretary at GE, and was talking about starting a family.

Although her husband looked good and had an engaging smile, I think he had been better at courting than at husbanding, but they did seem relatively happy. Dean may have smoked when he was younger, but he did not smoke after they were married, and, of course, my sister never smoked.

If the fifties life style had lasted forever, their life together would probably have been perfect, but by the late 60's that 50's optimism and affluence were being pushed aside by some mighty powerful new forces and beliefs. The major new beliefs seemed to center around the idea of equality, which reared its idealistic head in a number of areas as we all remember.

The Civil Rights movement was in full swing throughout the sixties. Someone noticed that a large segment of the American population was not sharing in "the good life". They often had no TV's and no cars in their possession; in fact they probably didn't even have a garage to put a car in. And even if they did, they could be, apparently, only "separate, but equal," not really equal. I don't think white Americans would have noticed this on their own, maybe they would have, but some Black Americans began to call attention to it.

TV made such a difference because it allowed events to be played out in our living rooms while we ate dinner, or prepared it, or got ready for bed, or when we woke up in the morning. It may have started out with Rosa Parks but it escalated into fire hoses and dogs and prejudiced southern "honkies" with "cracker" accents and mirrored sun glasses and Freedom Riders or Fighters, and deaths; four little girls in a church, some of the Freedom Fighters, eventually Martin Luther King. Many of us were aghast and could no longer pursue our middle class dreams until a few things got straightened out and the dream was not just for White America, but could be universal. How could we enjoy our affluent peace if images of injustice were going to march through our living rooms? (Of course, now we know there's not end to it, but we didn't know that then.)

And, of course, there was the war - the Vietnam War which was not World War II, global and morally necessary. It was a small local war in a totally foreign culture; a war many of us suspected was none of our business. Yes, the Cold War was in full swing, and yes, there was the question of the "red menace" sweeping in across the face of the earth, but didn't these people have the right to battle this out for themselves?

And it was such an awful war (all wars are awful) with such an elusive enemy. We often couldn't tell the enemy from the allies and we were not used to guerilla warfare tactics, hit and run battles. The jungle was so hot and dark and deep and so easy to get lost in, with natural enemies like bugs and snakes and rot to go along with the human opponents. And there was napalm and Agent Orange and reports of civilians ruthlessly murdered. It was an undisciplined, dirty war and we were not winning. America was in chaos and her citizens were far from home.

And then there was also women's liberation. Since everyone else was striving for equality, surely it was time to investigate the women's role in America. Were women to be a part of the "equal right's movement" or, if not, could they tolerate their position as "second class citizens" any longer. Women should get to live up to their full potential as human beings, either within the institutions of marriage and family, or outside of them, as necessary. Menial, repetitive housework and child-rearing tasks should not be the sole province of women, but should be shared by men, thus freeing women to satisfy higher needs, like the needs for an education, and a satisfying role in the world outside of the home, and to satisfy their sexual and spiritual needs. Why many women still lived in semi-slavery to dominating and despotic husbands!

And you can't forget the musical revolution and the pill. Of course, the musical earthquake began in the fifties with Buddy Holly, Elvis, et al. Add in the pill (the birth control pill) and pot, etc. and you get the heady mix of free love, getting high, grooving to heavy sounds and the promise of spiritual enlightenment right along with all that cultural equality. A new world order all rolled into one hit of astonishing power and excitement.

How did Felicity and Dean's little suburban paradise stand a chance against all this? We're a long way from cigarette smoking and addiction, you say? By now people were smoking funny cigarettes, wacky tabbacky. We're almost there.

Chapter 4

I Go To College

I graduated from high school in 1963. Snoopy was our class mascot. I had already done the PSAT thing and the SAT thing. No, I don't remember my scores; much higher in Verbal than in Quantitative, probably a great enough difference to constitute "scatter", if "scatter" is an issue with this test. "Scatter" apparently means some dark psychological forces may be at work in your psyche. (May explain a few things down the road.)

I was accepted by a four-year state university in a brutally cold little north country community, with the best fall weather anywhere, everything deep golden and russet with filtered sunshine and sunsets that drenched the sky with saturated color and all of it reflected in the river so that color was all around. It was just three hours from home but I felt, at the last minute, like I had been banished to Siberia instead of going off by choice to satisfy a lifetime goal. How could I leave everyone? I did it, I set my head straight forward and followed my nose, but I felt like a traitor, and a pioneer, and a victim of a terrible dismemberment. I knew that this parting was temporary, there would be vacations and semester breaks. But I also knew it was permanent, because I would go home as an outsider. I had thrown in my lot with the wide world and agreed to miss huge chunks of family history, which would take place without me.

I sent Mom and Dad home with my throat muscles clenched so tight against crying that I could barely breathe or speak and I went to college and had a great time.

I decided to major in English because it was my best subject. I had been discouraged about architecture by my guidance counselor after she saw my math test scores. Majoring in English does not prepare you for an actual career. To be practical I became an English Secondary Education major so that, if I had to, I could teach when I left school. What was I thinking? Of course I would have to teach when I left school. My family had no money and neither did I.

In my first year my roommates were music majors, nice girls, but they were never around, always practicing or performing or preparing for a performance. I was so lonely. I lost forty pounds from homesickness and from having a balanced diet for the first time in my life. Pasta and potatoes were no longer my major food groups. I discovered protein.

Typical dinners, *chez* Taylor, consisted of potatoes with hamburger gravy, potatoes with chipped beef gravy, macaroni and cheese (all of these recipes involved a roux, all were delicious, and all were way heavier on fat and carbos than they were on protein.) We also had spaghetti and meat balls, meat loaf and potatoes, beef stew, pot roast with potatoes and carrots and gravy, chicken and biscuits.

My mother lived through the Depression; she knew how to stretch a piece of meat. Later I had a boyfriend whose family had been migrant workers in the South and I learned about neck bones (which have even less meat than our gravies often contained) and red-eye gravy, which actually has no meat at all but uses burnt flour, so that it has a hearty, almost meaty taste. We used a lot of bullion in our household to enhance flavors.

We learned to make our own potato chips from real potatoes (which are delicious) and one of our biggest treats on a Sunday morning was to have fried dough with a variety of toppings. I preferred butter and salt, other family members preferred frosting or maple syrup or even jelly, or occasionally cinnamon and sugar.

So when I got to the dining room in college and was offered a whole steak instead of a small slice, I was pleasantly shocked. Our cafeteria offered only one meal a night and everyone had to make do with that one meal, like it or not. Our cooks were good though. In fact it was rumored that boys from the neighboring school dated girls from our school just to get invited to dinner. We had a huge cooler that offered all the milk and orange juice you could drink, no limit. By the time I left home to come to college "the big kids" at home were supposedly limited to one glass of milk a day and orange juice was a very rare commodity in our house. I don't remember what we drank before Kool-Aid, probably lemonade, but as soon a Kool-Aid came along we made several huge pitchers a day. Fizzies were also very popular at our house as we rarely had soda.

College food all by itself was therefore quite a culture shock to me. During my second year I had roommates from Long Island who ate things like blue fish and salmon, lobster, shrimp, clams, etc. One of my roommates actually had a summer house (well, her family did, although it was north shore, not south) where she went clamming frequently. I had never eaten any fish but fried haddock. Although we weren't Catholic, everyone in our town ate fried haddock. This was before fast food. This was about the only take-out you could get.

At college we all went out to restaurants at the drop of a hat, sometimes just for a snack after a movie, sometimes when someone's parents were visiting or if we were in town for an off-campus class. We learned to drink too. Sometimes it was 40 below zero for a week at a time. You had to warm up somehow. We played chugging games while our legs thawed out (girls wore skirts and dresses then). I never became a great drinker. Guess I don't have that gene, thank goodness.

You just learn so much at college that is not about course work. You learn other people's childhoods and customs; you learn to love things you never even heard of. I learned I had an extravagant streak. I loved things made of embroidered silk and real leather. I started to read through Mademoiselle and Vogue and Glamour, besides Look and Life. I learned about perfumes. One very stylish roommate introduced us all to the idea of men's colognes for women (4711, Canoe). Instead of Avon, I began to appreciate Givenchy.

Once I started to room with fellow English majors we became a bit more flamboyant and artsy. We edited the college yearbook and the literary magazine, went to poetry readings and took oil painting. We had boyfriends who were poets or actors. I had a folk singer from Ireland. We hung out at the coffee house. We were before the days of student demonstrations and sit-ins; at least they hadn't hit the North Country. We had curfews, and men and women had separate dorms. Almost every night a full contingent of fraternity brothers stopped by a dorm to serenade a girl who had gotten "pinned."

For the most part we didn't have cars and we walked everywhere we went until our junior and senior years when more friends with cars appeared on campus.

We studied hard. We usually went together to a study room across the quad from our dorm, a classically-dimensioned room with high windows, round tables and comfortable arm chairs in dark wood and fireplaces (not lit). We each took a separate table where we studied until almost curfew and then rushed home through the cold or shuffled home through the fallen leaves. We took breaks sometimes, in the snack bar upstairs where we could get orange juice and crushed ice to take back to our study table if we were in a time crunch. If we weren't in a hurry we would order coffee and vanilla ice cream, dip a spoonful of ice cream in coffee and slurp and talk about whatever, sometimes gossip, sometimes deep philosophical stuff. And we would smoke.

Yes, we all smoked cigarettes. My sophisticated friend of the men's-cologne-for-women trend, got French cigarettes in black cases that opened like a woman's compact. We were near the Canadian border. The cigarettes were oval, scented, and covered with pastel papers. For a while we all smoked these, but I soon settled on Parliaments and they became my cigarette of choice. I like the recessed filter. We could smoke or not smoke as we pleased in those days, because we did not inhale. We just puffed and looked mature and slightly jaded. So artistic. We were the Dorothy Parker Algonquin Round Table crowd of the North Country.

Our favorite movies were **Blow Up, The Americanization of Emily** and **Putney Swope**. I know that everyone was high in **Blow Up,** but I don't remember actually seeing anyone get high. These were the first hippies I ever saw, but I didn't know the word hippie yet. I don't remember if anyone smoked in the other two movies, but it didn't matter. Much more powerful influences than subliminal suggestion from movies were afoot.

I decided that, although I would probably have to teach for a living, I would have to live very large and have tons of experiences, even seamy ones, so that I could one day be a good writer. If you're supposed to write about what you know, then it would be best to know about everything.

Chapter 5

Tyler

Tyler's whole name is Tyler Hobart Taylor, which doesn't sound quite as bad as Tyler Taylor. All our names came right out of a Baby Names book. My parents were about two generations ahead of time when it came to picking out names

He may have been born with blond, curly hair, but he was always all boy. He would never play "house" or "wedding", but he would play "war" and "doctor" He was also available for "Hill Dill" or "Freeze Tag" or anything that involved running. When he got on the ice rink in the backyard it became a hockey rink. He was in favor of catching tadpoles, frogs, grasshoppers, and fire flies, cracking open rocks, burning things with a magnifying glass and doing anything involving a tool.

When we first moved to the country and we were after Dad to get us a swimming pool, Dad said, "Start digging" and left for work.

Tyler organized us all with shovels and we dug all day. When Mom objected, we told her that Dad told us to do it. By the time Dad got home from work we had made a rectangular hole, about 5' wide by 8' long by 1' deep, in the soft soil in the back corner of the yard. Dad couldn't say much, he blamed himself because we didn't understand sarcasm yet. He talked to Tyler and they went off and got a load of sand. The swimming pool became our sandbox where we spent many happy hours with trucks and various mud-cooking-baking duties.

Tyler built forts and rode bikes and learned to hunt and fish. He was the one who taught us all to play mumbley-peg and built a wall of the newspapers my father collected in the cellar to fire his BB gun into (until someone got hit in the leg.) He organized the baseball diamond games that stripped our front yard bare of grass, and the basketball court games that stripped the back yard of grass. Dad had a little farmer in him, but he never could get that grass to grow back until we were grown, even though the backyard was really just a meadow and not a lawn.

When Tyler entered his preteen years he became very self-conscious and stiff and full of guy-pride. When he had to go to the dentist, he let my mother go too but made her walk on the opposite side of the street. He made it clear that he was a bit embarrassed by it all.

He still had his coarse and playful side. He had to share a room with Robert and he considered Bobbie his personal plaything. Tyler farted in his face and then covered my little brother with a blanket to trap the noxious fumes. He called this "smotheration." He didn't just do this once, he did it many, many times. He also lit Bobbie's and his own farts with a lighter. To Felicity and me this all seemed disgusting and a very long way from Clark Gable.

It is a wonder our house did not burn down considering all of us going through our "fascination with fire" stage at different times.

In spite of these gaseous activities, Tyler wanted "the good life" which apparently, at that time, meant a cool car, an apartment, and a pretty girlfriend. He knew a lot about cars from all the time he spent hanging out under a car hood with my father, who kept any one of our procession of used cars running by performing some kind of magic under the hood.

When Felicity got her first car, the black VW Beetle, she didn't have her driver's license yet. Before she even got to drive her car, Tyler took it out for a joy ride with his friends and ended up rolling it several times in a field somewhere. Drinking was involved. He got out without a scratch, but the car was totaled.

As soon as he could after graduation he got a job repossessing cars, got a girlfriend with long blonde hair, got himself a red GTO with 4-in-the-floor, and rented an efficiency apartment on the best street in the city.

All was not smooth sailing in Tyler's world though. The blonde was balky. She broke his heart. The GTO transmission (which he installed) never was quite right, and the apartment did not turn out to be a chick magnet. But Tyler didn't burn his bridges with the family. He was home visiting all the time. Eventually he started going out with an auburn-haired, translucent-skinned beauty from his high school graduation class. Alison had a troubled family background, so they saved each other. Soon after they got married Tyler had to go to Vietnam.

Tyler smoked for many years. I think, when he was in Vietnam, he smoked things other than tobacco.

Chapter 6
Mary Crabtree

Even though our house was in the country, it was a transitional community. The old farms had been broken up and not all of the lots had been sold. A lot of older homes already occupied lots scattered here and there. Lots were larger than city lots, maybe ¼ to ½ of an acre. The roads were tarred, there were no sidewalks, and the leafy elms leaned out over the roads, lending shade and beauty. Ten years after we moved here, all the elms had to be cut down because of Dutch elm disease.

On one side of us lived an older couple who were Mennonites. We thought they were nice, but very strange. They had an old house covered in brown shakes, hidden behind many shrubs and pine trees. It looked like it belonged in Appalachia. They, "Aunt Annie" and "Uncle Kenny" could not cut their hair or have a TV, or listen to the radio. Their children were already grown and lived away. They had a huge garden in their back yard and canned their own vegetables. Uncle Kenny worked for the railroad. Sometimes Aunt Annie would invite us girls in to complete sewing projects and listen to religious lessons. For Halloween they gave out pumpkin cookies which we tried to trade off for candy until we found out how delicious they were. They raised a hedge against our back yard which allowed them pretty much total relief from the Taylor backyard mayhem.

On the other side of us was a tiny house that one could really only call a shack. It had been built at the back of a narrow, wet lot, so it was right next to our back yard. In this house lived a woman from our nightmares, Mrs. Crabtree.

Mrs. Crabtree definitely smoked and she drank, a lot. She never cut the grass in her front yard, and she would not let anyone else cut it either. Of course, she only had a front yard, so it gave the appearance that we lived next door to a vacant lot.
We really were scared of her, but we cut across her yard so many times to visit friends on her other side that we wore a path through the tall grasses. Usually the grasses were higher than our heads if we scrunched down a little.

35

Mrs. Crabtree was not sociable. She hardly ever left her house, that I remember, but always took deliveries, which must have cost a pretty penny, because we did not have many stores nearby. I guess once in a while she went somewhere in a cab.

We did see Mary Crabtree sometimes though, because living next door to her was sort of like living next door to a geyser. Periodically she would "go off". She would stand in her doorway with her flyaway head of dull ginger and gray hair, a cigarette in her hand or hanging from her bottom lip. She wore a full-length white slip for these occasions and she would start lecturing the neighborhood. She would sometimes spend half an hour or forty-five minutes reaming out everyone for all the injuries done to her since the last time she "went off".

Although by daylight we made fun of her, when the sun went down we weren't so brave and we were most often the subjects of her tirades. I'm sure she rued the day we arrived next door. She didn't know our names but she yelled at each of us individually, identifying us by our misdeeds. Many a dusk caught us all sticking pretty close to Mom and Dad and keeping a real, low profile while Mary did her thing. It never turned into one of those sweet stories where a child softens the grief and pain of an older person's life.

Once a trio of us was cutting across Mrs. Crabtree's front yard through the tall weeds when she jumped out of her door and yelled at us up close and personal. We turned tail and ran. After that we avoided her yard. Even as teenagers, when we played Hide and Seek in every other yard in the neighborhood, we avoided Mrs. Crabtree's yard so as not to touch her off.

Dad told us, when he thought we were old enough to understand, that Mary Crabtree was a WAC in WW II. He told us that she had a metal plate in her head. She drank to ease her pain and she yelled because she was so angry that when she got drunk, she finally let it all out. Dad sometimes did errands for her and tried to remind her that we did not break her windows on purpose, or yell just to ruin her naps (which was true because we were too scared of her). When she eventually got seriously ill, long after I was gone from the house, Dad drove her to the VA hospital where she lived out her days.

Mary Crabtree probably had nothing to do with my smoking addiction. She, actually, should have been a great smoking deterrent.

Chapter 7

S-E-X

When puberty hit everything changed. Once the hormone switch turns on, there's no turning it off again. My sister and I still played paper dolls, mostly we designed clothes for them, but instead of Betsy McCall paper dolls, we now went in for movie star/model types. We all still played football and baseball and shot baskets in the back yard, and we still played outdoor games. The difference is that we now preferred games where a boy had to touch you, or tackle you, or wrestle you. We much preferred to play after dark and we dropped "Hill Dill" for "Hide and Seek". We were very aware that these were coed activities. All of a sudden I became very self-conscious around neighbor boys I had taken for granted for years.

This is when I began to realize that, although I got some great "birth gifts", physical beauty was not one of them. I had to shop for my dresses in the "chubby" department, a nomenclature that, thank goodness is now obsolete. By the time I was fourteen I wore a 36C bra.

I was the only one in my gym class who wore a bra, so I hid almost inside my locker when we changed our clothes so that my ugly bra would not stand out among all the pretty undershirts. Probably everyone saw me and my bra any way, but I didn't know because I didn't look. I felt sloppy and awkward and clumsy. I spent hours looking in mirrors and picking at pimples on my face. I didn't have terrible acne, but I had the normal run of blemishes and blotches, some of which swelled to gargantuan proportions. Mostly I told myself over and over how ugly I was. Since that time I have learned that this is a teen-age rite of passage, but not every teenager suffers these symptoms to the same degree. I bet my sophisticated Long Island roommate never did. First of all, she was beautiful. Second of all she had a handsome, solicitous father who treated her like she was his princess.

When I was fourteen, I read Peyton Place, which I found at the library where I volunteered, and which I hid in a bottom desk drawer, under many papers, until I finished it. It was the first time I started to think about the sexual act itself, how it was done, how it felt, etc. I loved reading this book, but hated reading it too. While I was reading I would feel a certain heaviness, lassitude. My body would become hot and flushed and I would become extraordinarily aware of my body against the seat of the chair. If anyone entered the library, and very few people did, I would hide the book away in the desk drawer and pull myself back into the world of human interaction. At first I would resent them for interrupting my illicit biological moment, then I would gradually feel lighter and friendlier, the fourteen-year-old self I recognized.

After that I discovered my joy button and I spent a lot of private time at home pushing it. But I did not get any opportunities to have s-e-x with real boys. First of all, I was not ready for that. Although the idea of being kissed appealed to me, having sex with an actual man or boy did not occur to me. Second, no boys tried. I did not go out with any boys in high school at all. I was terribly shy at school. I did not even talk to boys except the ones in the neighborhood, and I spoke to them less and less frequently. I watched them; I developed a few long distance crushes, but none that were returned. I didn't even miss it yet, having a boyfriend. Apparently I would be what is known as a late bloomer.

When I wanted a partner for my sexual activities (such as they were), I just closed my eyes and a faceless man would appear. He was really just a vague male figure, broad shoulders, nicely dressed. I could not really undress him except for his shirt because I had never seen a grown man naked. I was still determined not to get married and ruin my life. But I did want to fall in love and I did want to know all about s-e-x. I had a long crush on Marty Zeferelli, but my best friend at the time decided she did too. She would embarrass me by writing notes to him. She told me that she told him that I liked him and I got so angry with her. Or we would gaze at him and giggle in the lunchroom. How junior high is this? And that's the age we were. We were only in eighth or ninth grade. Marty didn't like either one of us. He let us know by his nonverbal reactions that we were just an embarrassment. We were lucky he didn't decide to get revenge. And thus, without ever actually being in love I managed to have my first broken heart.

Books – now I love books and reading, don't get me wrong. I could immerse myself so completely in a book that it truly was like a time machine or a "place" machine. My present world and its circumstances would disappear. And in some ways this is a good thing, especially for a poor child. It definitely broadens your horizons and very inexpensively too.

But in other ways it can be unhealthy. For one thing, it can turn you into a sort of passive observer of life, one who stands back and watches, describes and analyses others, a person who is not a live-r of life. For another, it kind of makes you believe that things will happen to you with little or no effort on your part. Fictional characters can become more real then actual people. Everyone including one's self can become an archetype. Instead of learning your actual self, you may imagine and re-imagine yourself.

Life can happen like a story plot. Each "story" or segment of life can seem self-contained, with a beginning, middle, and an end. It can seem as if the events from one "story line" cannot affect the events in the next episode. Wrong!

I imagined myself as a heroic character, struggling to be larger than life. I would be as independent and smart and self-sufficient as Jo in **Little Women**, for example. Instead of working on me, I bemoaned my inability to be my heroine of the moment. Books and movies affected me so strongly. A book or a movie could move me to hysterical sobs and righteous anger about some injustice or personal pain experienced by a character. Or it might move me to tears of joy and brain waves of sunny optimism. I grew used to living other's lives instead of my own.

People gave our family boxes and boxes of books. Some were classics; most were bestsellers or Reader's Digest Condensed Books. I read more than anyone in my family and we were a family of readers. I read everything I could get my hands on, good, bad, or indifferent. I also saw every movie I could get to, except horror movies. After Tarantula I didn't bother with any more movies that I could only watch with my hands in front of my eyes. I don't even remember most of what I read. I do remember the **Bobbsey Twins**, which I read about a million times when I was seven. I remember **Nancy
Drew**. I also remember **Heidi**, **Alice in Wonderland** and **Through the Looking Glass** and "Archie" and "Superman" and "Spiderman" and **Treasure Island**.

I became aware of the world's injustices. When I read **The Diary of Anne Frank** and **Exodus,** I was aghast at the Holocaust. From **Inherit the Wind** and **To Kill a Mockingbird** I learned about narrow mindedness and prejudice. *West Side Story*, the sound track, which I learned by heart (and which everyone else in the family also learned whether they wanted to or not) brought **Romeo and Juliet**, ill-fated love, and gangs to life. My uncle had a book **The Last Days of Pompeii**, a chilling account of what it was probably like when the volcano buried Pompeii. Here was the awesome and malevolent power of nature. Life was deep. Everyday life, even s-e-x with real boys, could not hold a candle to this.

Not everyone in the family was so standoffish about S-E-X. I think by the time Felicity had graduated from high school and started in the community college, she was "doing it". And right upstairs in her new little bed-sitting room too. Tyler, I'm sure was doing it, and Gertie, well; we'll talk about that late. She was a whole other type of Taylor. But I wasn't anywhere near to doing the deed. Although I was privately titillated by it, I didn't even like to talk about it.

Then there was the whole issue of getting your "friend." I guess someone thought up that euphemism to put a positive spin on a sometimes-yucky fact of life. I got my "friend" when I was eleven, Felicity must have too because she already had hers when I got mine. And Gertie followed a couple of years later. There were no mini-celebrations in the Taylor household when you became a woman. Instead you inherited the "Welcome to Maturity" booklet (or whatever it was called) from the Kotex box to read, and Mom took you aside to communicate the hygiene essentials.

My father did all the shopping and he would bring home the giant economy sized box of Kotex. He must have been embarrassed, but he never mentioned it. We used paper lunch bags for disposal, so when you saw someone sneaking into the bathroom with their little lunch bag in hand you knew exactly what time of the month it was for them. Gertie loved to talk about her "friend" in excruciating detail, but I felt that it was not an appropriate topic for casual conversation. The less said about it the better.

I thought a lot about how nice it would be if women didn't have to have a period every month just so they could get pregnant if they wanted to. It seemed like overkill, biological redundancy, and a sad state of affairs for the female of the species. Not to mention that you could get pregnant when you didn't want to and that this could be very, very bad.

It would be nice if there was an on-off switch that you could make event specific, not the switch that turned on at puberty and off at menopause, but a switch that could be turned off and on at will. Maybe the switch could have a food trigger, off with chocolate, on with a jalapeno pepper, something like that. Of course you'd have to avoid chocolate when you wanted to get pregnant. That would be hard. But I assume that once the baby was planted you could go back to eating chocolate. I never did work out the fine points. Maybe someone has a better idea.

Anyway, with all these raging female hormones around the house, Tyler's injection of testosterone kind of got lost in the shuffle, except for some talk about facial hair and shaving and his rigid, zealous drive for privacy he couldn't get a word in edgewise.

In college, my sophisticated Long Island roommate had a boyfriend who went to school in Kentucky or Tennessee or somewhere south of the Mason/Dixon line. She ran up huge phone bills talking to him with her blankets pulled over her head. The college was crowded; we were three to a room. But I never heard a word of her romantic conversations. With 500+ girls in one dorm and the Beatles playing top force up and down the hallways, girls dancing, talking, setting or ironing each other's hair, or arguing, it was impossible to hear much. I didn't mind it, I was used to chaos, but when I had to study I usually had to leave the dorm. Did you remember that Audrey Hepburn smoked? So did most of the girls in my dorm. We didn't know from second-hand smoke.

I went out on my first dates in college. I was thinner, I had fashion consultants now, and I had my hair colored blonde and cut in a new mod style. One of my memorable dates was with a very cute guy with a suction kiss. He was a great kisser; he connected right from the mouth to the joy spot. I only went out with him once. He never asked again. Probably he had expected more from his hard work. But it taught me what I could expect from a good kiss. It raised my standards. By senior year I had met my Irish folk singer and my best friend had hooked up with his actor friend, and the four of us hung out. We went to the coffee house a lot so Ian could play and sing with the other folk singers. Ian's uncle was our Irish Lit. Professor and Ian took us to his uncle's house sometimes, where we could sit in front of the fire and drink Irish coffee. I loved the idea of Ian.

The World's Fair was in Montreal that year so we went. Ian flirted throughout the trip with my best friend. We had arranged it so I would spend the night at Ian's apartment instead of at the dorm, but I was so angry (?scared) from all the flirting that I wouldn't. Thus ended my first real relationship. I fled home where I was treated to a mini-makeover and antidepressants and arrived back at college in time to graduate. Still a virgin.

I'm sure you're wondering what all this has to do with my cigarette addiction. Well I will tell you that my initiation into the mysteries of inhaling and sexual intercourse happened at almost the same instant.

Chapter 8

Gertrude

Gertie, as I have said, was a different kind of Taylor altogether. She did not care about excelling in school. She was content to do OK in basic courses. She didn't bother to join our sorority. She just wanted to have a good time. She would lower her lashes and smile until her dimples showed and make everyone around her feel, with happy certainty, that some flirty mischief was about to take place.

In childhood she played the same things we all did. She was best friends with the two younger sisters across the street and usually did not bother to tag along with Felicity and me. She liked "jump rope" and "hopscotch" and "Mother-May-I". She liked roller-skating and dresses.

As soon as puberty hit she got a shape that was designed to make boys crazy, with large breasts and a tiny waist. She wasn't perfect. She had the bad complexion we all had either from heredity or poor nutrition.

Gertie's best friends after puberty were not the popular kids, they were the rebels, the James Deans, the hood types, the boys with leather jackets and duck tail haircuts, the girls with reputations for being fast. They didn't do wild and anti-social acts, but they were into action. They loved to play records and dance and probably smooch, although I can't be sure because I didn't hang out with them very often. Smithvale had grown into the type of small town where teens took long evening walks and met friends or went to the little league ballpark to hang out near the Babe Ruth game. Gertie met her friends at street corners, enjoying herself so much that she didn't want to come inside. Her gifts were social.

Gertie was also very earthy, didn't mind coming home with a hickey now and then, or talking to anyone about every detail of her bodily functions. Probably Mom and Dad worried about Gertie the most. She was the most likely candidate in the family so far to end up in the dreaded "pregnant out of wedlock" state. They didn't worry too much though because, for the most part, it looked like she just knew how to party, something the rest of us were not particularly good at.

We all had our little square cases with musical notes on the sides to organize and carry our 45's- our "Teen Angel", "Bye-Bye Love", Wake Up Little Suzie", Blue Suede Shoes", and "Love Me Tender". Felicity kept hers in alphabetical order. No two records could go in the same space and every title was written into the appropriate space on the index card inside the cover of the box. The front section held those little plastic adapters that had to be snapped into each record so it could be placed on the skinny record player spindle.

I wasn't quite so neat about my little record box, but I was neater than Gertie. She put her records in order from most favorite to least favorite, but since the order was always changing, she couldn't write anything in the index or on the tabs at the top of the dividers. You could never find anything in her 45 box, but she knew all the new dance steps. She knew how to slop and jitter bug, and how to do the mashed potatoes, and the jerk, and the twist. And she knew how to do the dog, which Felicity and I considered too gross to even look at.

Gertie's values were somewhat different from the rest of us also. Once amid a succession of older station wagons, Dad, in an attempt to find a car that would fit the whole family comfortably, fell heir to an antique extended-body Packard in black. It had about 3 feet of carpet between the front seat and the back seat. On the back of the front seat were two small, upholstered seats that folded down and held extra passengers. This car had obviously once graced a life of affluence and luxury. It still looked really good. Most of us appreciated the luxurious provenance of the car and enjoyed riding in it. Especially since we didn't have to have two layers of kids in the back seat and for some reason throwing up was no longer an issue.

This voluptuous old Packard, however, mortally embarrassed Gertie. To her it was just a monstrosity. The car did have one serious flaw. It had a cracked engine block, which soon made its presence known. If we went too far or climbed too many hills the car would overheat and we would have to pull over and wait until the engine cooled before we could complete our outing. Then we would all pile out of that car like clowns from a Volkswagen. Gertie knew what was cool, and this humiliating routine, on top of the unusual look of the thing was too much for her to accept. After my father had to order her into the car a few times, and after several episodes of impassioned, tearful refusal, Dad gave up on the Packard, which would never have made it through the winter anyway, and got a more conservative and more modern junker. A few of us were quite disappointed to see the old Packard go though.

Gertie married right out of high school. She "picked up" her husband-to-be at a downtown movie theater. He was stationed at the local air base, which still existed, but was much smaller than it had been just after World War II. He was with a friend and he started pestering my sister and her girlfriend. I made the two of them move to another seat. The young men followed. Finally I left the four of them giggling and chatting and sat in another part of the theater.

After the movie we waited out on Main Street. Gertie was still at it, flirting and dancing the dog, right there on Main Street. I told Dad when he came to pick us up. I'm sure Gertie did not love me very much at that moment. Jason, the young air force guy, invited himself to dinner at our house and proceeded to charm Dad, who never did feel he had enough sons. They had a fairy tale marriage through fourteen years and two sons until Jason's philandering ways became too obvious to ignore. He broke Gertie's heart, big time. Actually he broke all of our hearts.

Gertie never smoked, (well she may have tried it once or twice). Jason did.

Chapter 9

Robert

Felicity was the first child, me, Zoe, the second, Tyler, the third, and Gertie the fourth. Robert was #5. Before puberty Robert was a victim to Tyler, and a baby doll to Felicity, Gertie and me. We felt bad when Tyler tortured him with the old "smotheration" routine. At first we told mom, who did the "wait until your father comes home" bit. Dad always did his duty in these situations, but his heart wasn't in it. And afterwards Tyler might torture Robert even more with psychological insults against his courage or his gender. Tyler didn't torture Robert everyday anyway. There were lots of days when they got along great, but because of the age difference Robert would always be the follower and Tyler the reluctant and twisted mentor.

Felicity and Gertie and I just loved Robert. He was our first baby. He came along when we were old enough to do some nurturing, holding a bottle, watching Mommie change his diaper, or finding the "blankie" (Robert rubbed the satin on a certain blankie until he was about five and it consisted of only a few threads, crisscrossed and fuzzy). Next thing you know he was a toddler waddling along behind us with blankie, and so cute. He had a little tough face and a blond crew cut, and he smiled with his whole face. He would do anything we asked, even be the groom when we played wedding with the youngest of the three sisters from across the street. He was our pet. Tyler had Pete, the dog, but we had our cat Bootsy and we had Robert.

After puberty Robert was never a victim again. He discovered beer early and was addicted early. He had an informal posse of cohorts, all boys, who also pledged allegiance to beer and to feats of drunken courage. Most of Robert's friends were nice boys from around Smithvale, who appreciated his creativity and Bobby was truly inspired, leading his merry band from one humorous and borderline illegal adventure to the next. Their deeds were legendary and sometimes noisy. Robert had a whole room to himself by his teenage years because the rest of us older siblings were no longer in the house. I was still in college and came home for weekends and school breaks and summers.

Robert's room in our house was called the "Sin Den". If you opened the door, which you did only after gaining clearance, clouds of cigarette smoke would greet you, along with crashing music, beery exhalations and an explosion dirty underwear. State your business and go. But Robert also had a roguish charm that allowed him to pass all this off as just testosterone, high spirits, and boyish humor.

Robert also had a corner of the basement for his drum set, which was the height of generosity and parental love on the part of my mother. She had never appreciated music of any kind, to her it was all noise, and the drums were parked right next to her escape hatch, her laundry area. The boys knew how to get around Augusta though. They flattered her and teased her, made her laugh, and flirted with her. It wasn't even just a strategy to get away with things. Those boys truly loved her, sort of adopted her. They often stayed to dinner; they ran away to our house, slept off drunks at our house and hardly ever went home as far as I could see. Sometimes their moms were jealous but they certainly knew my mom wasn't trying to steal their children.

Robert and his "posse" did things like sneak into the E. J. Strodel Warehouse, take cases of beer out into the woods behind the warehouse, and get someone to take them back later to load up the beer and take it to wherever they hid it. After I got my car, I did a couple of beer runs when I was home from school, but I had no guts for this kind of caper at all.
A few times I accompanied the boys to Scruples Bridge, a tall truss bridge over a local river. They would climb to the very top, bolstered by alcohol and jump into the river. After I heard that, historically, boys had died when they hit rocks hidden under the water, I didn't take them anymore. I'm sure they just found another ride.

Robert was the first Taylor to attract the attention of the police. This is the only thing that he did that really devastated mom. The idea of having a police car parked in our driveway for the whole world to see was more than she could bear. I guess Bobby had been talked into being lookout for a new friend whose misdeeds went well beyond those of Robert and his friends. He got off with a warning, went back to his old friends, and was never in trouble with the police again.

Bobbie was elected president of ZEUS fraternity in high school and the rumors of their exploits made him the darling of the high school for at least his senior year. One exploit apparently involved no pants and a snow bank. These same exploits were probably to blame for the demise of sororities and fraternities at our high school. Robert was extremely shy about girls, but my younger sisters reported that girls were forever trying to catch his attention at school, waving coy "hi, Bobbie's" in his directions.

The dark side of Robert, however, was the way he passed on the Taylor male tradition of torture to my younger sisters. He and his boys would often fill up the living room and my sisters, who arrived home later, had to run the gauntlet in order to enter the house. The guys had long derogatory nicknames for each of my sisters. Emily, Rebecca, and Morgan still remember these long chains of derision and can recite them to this day. For the boys, the entire object of the exercise was to entertain themselves and to force the girls from the living room so the guys could have it. Although my sisters tried to hang tough, eventually someone would run crying or in anger from the room and the rest would follow to give comfort. Emily was the one most frequently reduced to tears.

My younger sisters did many of the same fun things the rest of us had done in their early childhood years, and they got to go places with my parents more often, because there were no more babies, but their youthful pleasures were marred by the torment they had to endure to get through the living room each day, or anytime the guys wanted to evict them from any space, or anytime those bozos wanted to boost their egos with a little bullying. To realize that some of this was payback for the times Robert was tortured by Tyler would not exactly require the services of a psychotherapist.

I witnessed several examples of the dreaded "dinner table torture". My dad was working nights at this time. He went off to work before dinner. My brother hoarded all the food and would not pass it until you either asked for the item in Spanish with an accent that perfectly matched his original pronunciation, as in '?Pase me le leche por favor', or sometimes he made up an arcane enunciation that had to be duplicated, like gra-VEE for gravy. My mother tried to control him, but he would turn on his charm (he could be very funny) until he made her laugh, or they would get into a mock slapping fight and mom would eventually crack up and retreat. Dad would hear about an incident, but it just sounded like horseplay to him. Robert never did any of this when dad was home.

Once Emily, Rebecca, and Megan hit high school age, the boys did not tease them as much and some of them started flirting with the girls, especially Becky, who was our family's only long-legged blonde. But it was too late. My sisters despised Robert's friends, although later, as adults, they forgave them.
I think you can guess that Robert smoked, a lot. He smoked until his late twenties or early thirties. When he started to cough up blood, he stopped. He had to choose between the beer and the cigarettes. His beer addiction won out over his cigarette addiction

Chapter 10

Falling in Love Inappropriately

You would think that graduating from college with high honors, as I did that summer of 1967, would mean that I was mature and smart. I did have a head full of knowledge and a heart full of the desire to be an excellent high school teacher. I also had a job in September at a high school in a well-to-do neighborhood where I expected to find ambitious dedicated students.

Okay, we've already established that books aren't everything, but I was so inspired, so bursting with the beauty of language and literature and the cosmic connections between human history, art, music, and language, that I felt as if I had swallowed the Milky Way. My excitement beamed from me. I was incandescent. We didn't know anything about "Emotional IQ." Mine was probably about equal to that of a sixteen year old.

And that's who I hung out with that summer after college ended and before I started teaching, sixteen year olds. My brother Robert had a new friend, Luke, who was attracted by the drums that Bobby banged away on in the basement next to the washing machine and dryer. Luke looked like a Liverpool, England boy with dark blond hair fringing his handsome face. He was a naturally smart kid, but destined for blue-collar physical labor. Many a woman's life has probably been derailed by an inappropriate love interest. Not a new story, but for someone who was supposedly headed out into the wide adult world, it can bring progress to a screeching halt, make you want to stay in the moment.

That June I spent many hours talking to Luke while we sat in my turquoise Chevy Impala convertible at the end of my parent's street, watching the planes take off and land. We talked about what we wanted and what we believed, but it was really all about attraction, hormones, pheromones; chemistry. I don't know what Luke felt, I never asked. I assumed the pleasure he took in my company was not purely intellectual, was visceral and chemical, like mine. I think an attraction must be mutual for it to generate this much energy. I waited all day for the evenings in the car watching the smoky blue lights that lined the runways and feeling pretty smoky blue myself. That June I was only alive when we were together and I was oblivious to social embarrassment, parental disapproval, all of it. It was all pretty innocent after all. In spite of my obsession I was passive, waiting for the first move to come from Luke. All we did was talk.

In July Luke suggested that I could get an apartment with his sister Lena, who was ready to move away from her parents and needed a roommate. I liked her, she was alive, somewhat witty, and so full of self-confident energy that she was positively loaded with an earthy charisma. She had not gone to college and she had already been married and divorced. Even so she was younger than me. She also had blonde hair, and a full, sensual face and figure.

There were whispers that she was a "homosexual". I was incredulous, never having given a thought to such a predilection. (I didn't even know about Rock Hudson.) I decided it was just small town gossip. I hated gossip. It was like those tacky "True Confessions" magazines we all passed around in our teens that recounted the tales of the million ways an unsuspecting girl could lose her reputation. "My Baby's Father Beats Me", My Baby's Father is My Father" and other horrific permutations of the victimization of women by men. It never dawned on me that a woman could be loved or victimized by another woman. That's how sheltered my beginnings were.
So the adventure began. We moved into the "city," the same city my family had left thirteen years earlier. The city had a university, so it had a university neighborhood. How hip. The apartment was at the top of an older apartment building that had five other apartments. It was a gray clapboard structure and the apartment was not awful, a one bedroom with a nice porch off the living room. The rooms were good sized, there were lots of windows. I felt good about it.

Then Lena introduced me to her girlfriend, Ivy, and I understood that the rumors were true. I would be tolerant, I decided. I wanted to experience everything life had to offer and I wanted a place to visit with Luke away from prying eyes. It would be good to learn about lesbians. It shouldn't make any difference who we love. I didn't want to have a "lesbian experience" of my own, but this should not be a problem. Lena was obviously in love with Ivy, who was a thin, shy likeable young black woman. Luke would be around a lot too after all, and school would keep me very busy.

It was a disaster. Lesbianism was the tip of Lena's unconventionality iceberg. She did not have any serious career plans. She did sort of want to play house with Ivy, but that did not mean she wanted to make curtains, or buy knickknacks. They were always in the car off to somewhere, usually Lena's mom's house. I wasn't really clear about why she left her mother's house to begin with. I guess it was because sleepovers weren't allowed.

Lena was also into drugs. She smoked cigarettes, of course, but she also smoked marijuana. She had some kind of menial job, at a potato chip factory or something. When she got home, she got high while she waited for Ivy and then took off. Sometimes Luke would come over with his boys and they would also get high. I puffed my cigarettes, but I would not smoke marijuana.
Lena, it turned out, was an expert at abuse and manipulation. She knew how to take a weakness and tweak it. If you had an insecurity, she knew how to use it to her advantage. God help you if she wanted something from you and you were unwilling to give it. She was ruthless in her pursuit of absolute personal satisfaction.

Fortunately for me, she didn't concentrate on me. She had Ivy. Ivy was not "out". Her family had no idea of her inclinations. She had some big bruiser brothers who would not be happy. They even daunted Lena. This did not keep her, however, from exploiting Ivy's fears of discovery in order to keep Ivy at heel. Ivy was very unhappy. Lena was way more than she bargained for, noisy, aggressive, not at all into nesting. I think Ivy wanted to settle down, come home from a day of nursing, put up her feet, and bask in the glow of someone who loved her. Lena loved her possessively and assertively, but had no immediate interest in settling down.

They fought constantly, Ivy quietly and stubbornly, Lena raging off into the night. Before the summer was even over I had had it. I told Lena I was moving out. I found an ad in the paper. Some girls in a flat needed a roommate. I went for an interview. Beautiful old flat on a tree-lined street right outside of a green city park with a big pool and a rose garden. The middle bedroom was empty. The living room had a fireplace, the kitchen a breakfast nook. There was a deep front porch along the front of the house.

Two local girls who worked for downtown stockbrokers lived there already. We all liked each other. I could move in at the end of the month. Lena and I had a month-to-month rental so I did not have to worry about breaking a lease. Once Lena and Ivy broke up, Lena didn't mind moving back home again.

I had to go to my college roommate's wedding on Long Island. Lena wanted to see her ex-husband and her uncle in New York City. She wanted to get some money from her uncle and her ex. Luke would go too, they would stay with their uncle while I went to the wedding. Lena and I still got along. This was OK with me. I liked to be anywhere Luke was. I just didn't want to live with Lena.

Her ex-husband had decided that he was a musician. He was so hip he was scary. Thin, with spiky black hair and a leather jacket, he did reveal a continuing fondness for Lena. He lived in a disgusting apartment on Avenue C in the Village, crawling with cockroaches, with a dirty bathtub in the kitchen. A lot of joints were smoked, but there was no money here to spare. We went uptown to Uncle Chet. He lived in a rent-controlled building on Lexington. The elevator smelled like strawberries, it smelled like patchouli everywhere else. He was Lena's gay uncle and his place was beautifully decorated in a toned-down mod style. He was an educated and amusing man, just nearing middle age, living on his own at the moment. He was "somebody" and he knew "people".

It was hard to contain Lena's energy in such an upholstered space but her uncle was genuinely fond of her and indulgent. I left to go to my exotic roommate's wedding.

From all this immense culture shock I took enormous, although not uncomplicated, pleasure.

The paradoxes in my life totally parallel the extremes in this trip to New York City, from sleazy, to artsy, to upscale, my life would run the gamut. After the "moseltov" at the wedding I found myself at a huge banquet restaurant in Rockaway, mingling with Long Islanders in long dresses and their best coiffures at table after table of hor'd'oeuvres. These appetizers, which I thought to be the whole wedding spread, proved to be a prelude to a luxurious sit-down dinner followed by a dessert cart from nirvana. We danced the Hora, I saw all my old friends from college, and the beautiful bride who never married the Kentucky boyfriend at all, but ended up marrying a podiatrist from Chicago.

I did not crave her life, or think about hanging on in Long Island. Of course I had my teaching job to go back to, but you would think, given my big dreams in life, I would have tried to hitch my star to these winners. Never gave it a thought. Their background was too different from mine. This was their world. I was off back to mine. I couldn't wait to begin. I was scared to death to begin. Summer was over. I had a new place to live. I was out from under the cloud of Lena (I thought) and could just enjoy the energy of Lena. I was ready to go. I still didn't inhale.

Chapter 11
Teaching

America was going wild. Everywhere was protest and upheaval, boundaries being pushed past their limits in heady growth spurts of positive energy and negative energy, a tug of war for the future of the American culture. It was a rush, and many of us seemed swept along with a current of change that was exhilarating or crushing, depending on the issue and your previously held beliefs.

Guilt was bubbling over the fires of America. End the war, end American "apartheid", end the raping of the earth, and stop pigging out on the earth's finite resources.

No more women as "second class citizens", we were freed by the birth control pill to take charge of our destiny. Once our bodies were free we could free our minds and our spirits. We could become cultural warriors, along with our men, like our Amazonian forbears. We could go out and conquer the canyons of our great cities.

But danger was also afoot. While heroes were being made, our greatest leaders were being assassinated, right here in America. When Kennedy was shot, I was downtown in our little northern college town shopping with my roommates. We were just about to enter the jewelry store, which was broadcasting a radio station in the entryway near the display windows. When we heard the so-shocking news we left downtown immediately, in tears, and arrived back at the dorm to sit with all our friends in the lounge and see the fifties end in 1963 on national television. The pink and navy suit that Jacqueline wore – the funeral cortege – John Jr., manly little toddler, holding his mother's hand and saluting his dad. Our president murdered.

Yin and yang – who knew that we Westerners would suddenly need the comfort of Eastern religion to understand events in the "land of the free", the "home of the brave". Black panthers, right fists knuckled and raised proudly, "Black Power", sent shivers down the spine of white America, both of fear and of pride.

Buses were loaded to go to Washington to protest the war, more buses to protest segregated schools or school bussing, more buses to fight for the rights of women, and even more buses to protest the protesters. The buses rolled out with the brave radical or reactionary souls to fight the good fight or protect the status quo. There was fear in this. Something could go wrong, you could end up in jail or dead. There was camaraderie in this, solidarity with a community of like-minded contemporaries. Usually Martin Luther King's example of peaceful civil disobedience held sway, perhaps diverting serious bloody rage-outs. We owe him.

The SDS, college campus heroes staged sit-in, be-ins. Our fathers and mothers who were in charge of our institutions were stunned, uncomprehending, angry. They fought back, and when slammed by massive outrage, reluctantly agreed to change.

Music was also gone mad, Bob Dylan, who could have said it better? It was all happening to a beat,: from Motown, "Baby Love, Oh Baby Love', "R-E-S-P-E-C-T", from space, "Light My Fire", from Liverpool, "Eleanor Rigby", "Norwegian Wood", from the west coast, "I Get Around", and from another planet, 'Blowin' in the Wind." The beat was the bass that underlined each day and pounded the whole glorious adventure into our "collective unconscious."

In the midst of this I had to move into my new apartment and start my first year of teaching. But I had smelled marijuana, I had seen our president shot, I had seen Tyler off to war in Vietnam, and all my 50's security was toppling.

Two weeks into my first semester of teaching I knew I was in deep shit. It wasn't going well. I had two classes of ninth grade English and two of tenth. These were not the goal-oriented, studious young people I had invented. They drew the battle lines. Last year they got rid of two teachers, they said, this year they were shooting for four. I planted my high heels. I wasn't going anywhere. It was war. But I didn't have a discipline gene.

We did study English, but I took such an academic approach that I lost them, or maybe they were just too intent on sabotage. We did some good stuff, we did anti-utopias, **Animal Farm** and an offshoot writing assignment. We did "The Lottery" by Shirley Jackson and "The Sniper" by Liam O'Flaherty. We did poetry, haiku, Shakespeare and grammar. We did a unit on Civil Disobedience, Henry David Thoreau and Gandhi, but my classroom was unusually chaotic. We had a whirl-I-gigs siege which involved the construction of dozens of notebook paper whirl-I-gigs which somehow appeared mysteriously on the ground under my windows in the courtyard.

I often had to shut my classroom door because other people complained about the noise. Once my tenth graders planned a B-B attack. Ten minutes into the class I was bombarded with copper B-B's. I was rolling around on them. They were pinging against the blackboard. I did, at least, stand in front of the classroom door just before the bell rang and tell my darlings they couldn't leave until the B-B's were all picked up. I had to write a lot of passes, which I refused to do. I eventually had to relent because students without late passes had nothing to do but roam the halls. I should have reported them all, called their parents. No one had given us an arsenal of techniques for dealing with classroom war. I was embarrassed. If I gave detention, then I had to manage the perpetrators in the after school detention room. There was obviously more to this teaching stuff than knowing your subject matter.

My department chair, Mitchell Gerard, was a distinguished gentleman and a beloved teacher. He called me into his office several times. He summarized for me what was going on in my classroom , which I already knew quite enough about, but he gave me no ideas about where to go from there. Teacher's classrooms are their domains. Perhaps he didn't want to interfere. There was also a social studies teacher, Mr. Boyd. He tried to convince me to relax and not take it all so seriously. He spirited me away to a local cider mill during my first period each day, which was a planning period, for coffee and donuts. We weren't supposed to leave the building, but no one really cared. He sort of bucked me up to face each new day. My mom sometimes shared her Librium with me, when I totally lost courage. I had never failed before at academics.

Part of the problem, I reasoned, was that my students were way ahead of me emotionally. Their parents were young and had way too much money. They worked a lot and they went out a lot. The kids would meet at a home where parents were absent and they were free to drink, smoke, party, and experiment with sex every night. The girl's classroom attire was outrageous. They wore short, short skirts with garters which showed below their hemlines and which were fastened to their stocking. I had never encountered this style of dress before, and have not since. The school did not disallow it. They were not at all ladylike about the way they sat. I tried to talk to them about the pitfall of living their lives to please men, but they weren't buying it.

The boys were flirtatious and pretended to be in love with me. I finally did several lessons on courtly and unrequited love. I received several illuminated medieval love scrolls. I complimented the artists and this trend died out.

I had one young student who, although bright, would not hand in any assignments. He would only hand me, each time, a sheet of paper that read "I'm Jimmy Carl Black, I'm the Indian of the group." This, I eventually learned could be credited to the Mothers of Invention of "Boobs-a-lot" fame. He said he did this to get his father's attention.

It wasn't working with his father. He certainly had my attention though. Although we talked to his parents, threatened to drop him from the football team and eventually did drop him from the football team, he stubbornly remained "Jimmie Carl Black" for the entire school year. Except for his refusal to complete a single school assignment he had a delightful personality and was very popular.

I made it through the year and then resigned. I thought that perhaps my lack of "life experience" made it difficult to manage a classroom with the perfect blend of compassion and sternness. I was relieved, but also deflated. Perhaps if I wasn't still a virgin when the year began; perhaps if I had learned to inhale sooner?

Chapter 12

Augusta

Now I know that so far my portrait of my mother has been less than flattering, but that's just because I have different goals from my mom. Her goal in life was to marry and have a family. She accomplished exactly what she wanted to accomplish. I can't help it if it looked to me like the third ring of Dante's **Inferno**.

She met my dad when she was nineteen through a group of mutual friends. From the beginning he was the only one for her. It was the middle of the Depression. Neither of Dad's parents had jobs, Dad supported them. He didn't know how to stop. My mother waited six years to marry my dad. As soon as they married, Dad's parents got divorced and went to work. He probably should have cut them loose sooner.

Augusta was working in an office as a secretary. When Hobart married her she was twenty-five years old. Hobart was thirty. She worked days; he worked nights. For the first two years of marriage Augusta, on her way to work, waved from the bus window to Hobart as he drove home from work in the early morning. After two years of hardly seeing each other, as soon as they were in the same place at the same time, they started their family. They had one, two, three, four babies right in a row, two not even a whole year apart. Two years later the fifth baby appeared and they made the move to Smithvale.

Our city apartment seemed to be always neat and well organized. In our pictures we wore starched and ironed dresses and hair dos with ribbons. Mom told us that she did not know how to cook at all when she married, that she burned the pan the first time she tried to boil water. I remember when the pressure cooker blew up and spat potatoes all over the ceiling. I don't know how cooking could have eluded her because she came from a very poor family, but apparently her mom did all the cooking. Although she lost track of what was cooking on the stove and burned things, by the time the oldest of us were in our teens, when she could pay attention, she was a pretty good cook.

In Smithvale, for some reason, Augusta's housework often got the better of her. Having three more babies certainly could have done it. She just could not keep up with it all. Her floors were mopped or swept, her sinks, toilets, etc. were clean, but she just did not seem able to throw anything away. Things piled up.

Having a spotless house, however, is not necessarily a hallmark of great mothering. Augusta was a great mother.

When they tarred our road one hot summer day, after we all walked in the tar with our bare feet, Mom lined us all up on the back stairs and patiently cleaned our feet with Lestoil and then filled a tub with water for us to rinse our feet in. She didn't rant and rave about her floors, none of us even made it inside. She didn't spoil our fun. Our moods were just as good with clean feet as they had been when we were glorying in hot tar. We liked our clean feet and didn't go back out to the tar either.

When anyone was sick, they got to lie in state on the living room couch all day and Mom made sure there was ice cream and/or ginger ale if they were up to it. If everyone was sick she was a tireless nurse. Her hand on your forehead felt like healing. We had measles, chicken pox, whooping cough, and some of us had mumps. It would take a long time from the time the first child got sick until the last child got well. In those days they felt it was good to expose everyone while they were young and let them get over it, not they we had any space to isolate someone anyway. We all made it through all of those childhood diseases.

Sometimes all the other neighborhood mothers came over and sat around in the back yard or the dining room. We couldn't help hanging around to listen to them. The discussion always got around to childbirth, each mom trying to outdo the other with length of time in labor and other grueling details of blessed nativity. Augusta had a hard time competing. Once she was in labor for twenty minutes. She tended to have very small babies, 3 lbs 10 oz, 4 lbs 3 oz. When she had a six pounder it was considered huge. Even the small babies were completely formed and healthy although two of her babies had to stay in the hospital for at least a month after they were born. She wasn't just a great mother; she was a lucky mother.

Hobart was a practical man. He handled all the money. If we needed something and he knew we didn't have enough money, he believed we would just have to do without. Augusta, who had gone without more often than not, didn't agree. Shoes were always a big issue and Augusta saw to it that we always got them. Hobart was forced to perform lots of budgetary magic over the years but he generally came through, or Butch (that was what everyone, ironically, called mom) would nag him to death.

Augusta found time to join the PTA, to make cookies and cupcakes and cakes to send to school, to assist in a Brownie troop, and to take in extra kids to baby-sit for when money was tight, which was always. Even when we were grown we called Mom several times a week and everyone came back home every Sunday with husbands, kids, dogs, and relatives.

The girl across the street, Carrie, who was Robert's age and had only one older brother, hated to go home. She had a spotless, beautifully decorated house to go home to. She also had a mom who never stopped yelling. And her mom and dad never stopped fighting. They drank and, of course, they smoked and screamed, a lot. We had to practically throw her out of our house. And Augusta hated to do that, but was more afraid of a tongue-lashing from Carrie's "straight-talking" ("b" word) mom.

I guess I would have to say that our mom, Butch had a gift. It was a gift for making a family and for making anyone who visited us feel like a temporary member of the family. When we went on a picnic, we always made a huge group with softball games and lots of food and laughter. Even when we went somewhere as simple as the Little League baseball field (which took the place of the old barracks the fire fighters used to burn) everyone we knew came along, like a long neighborhood parade, the biggest "family" at the ballpark.

They say about daughters that we all become our mothers. Even though I swore that what Augusta wanted was not what I wanted, even though I still did not want to be a housewife and a mother, I spent the next twenty years of my life trying to mold all the disparate groups of people who populated my life into one family after another. And because of Augusta's excellent example, I was often able to succeed in creating or joining close nurturing groups of strangers, in spite of the fact that I had no idea that this was my goal.

Chapter 13

The Apartment by the Park

I moved in with my new roommates just before school started, the only great decision I made. If I was still trying to deal with Lena's nonsense, along with getting through that first disheartening year of teaching, I probably would have been certifiable.

Linda had the front bedroom, which was obviously built to be the master. It was the largest of the three bedrooms and she furnished it with some style from second hand furniture stores. Linda was from an eastern suburb (Smithvale was north of the city) known for its affluence and good schools. Her family, however, was not well off. They were a big Irish family with seven children and she was the oldest. She had long hair and a thin angular face and a little boy's body, straight up and down, but she still managed to look confident, stylish, and arrogantly intelligent. She had heavy Modigliani style upper eyelids, which were her best feature. She was brisk and practical and wittily waspish, hard to warm up to. She had to wear thick-lensed glasses much of the time. She had an architect boyfriend who had the upstairs flat in the house next door. Most of these houses had been built within the same era and were almost identical except for the exterior color and landscaping.

The architect's name was Peter. He was older than we were, in his thirties. He had long hair, which was just becoming the style at the time, and a stocky, very slightly overweight body. He was always brushing his hair off his face, but he had very kind eyes, and although he had the same dry wit as Linda he also had an air of languid ennui that seemed very mature. He was usually fatherly and friendly and stayed out of our roommate squabbles. He loved jazz, had a very expensive sound system. He used a bed for a sofa and covered it with a genuine cowhide throw and with many huge pillows. He loved to prop you comfortably among the pillows with some excellent headphones and select some John McLaughlin or Miles Davis for you to listen to. He was never called Pete. Some people are nickname people, some aren't. Peter wasn't.

I had the middle bedroom, which, like the first bedroom had two huge windows that started about 12" off the floor and went almost all the way to the ceiling. The windows were in the center of a wall with about 6" between them. On the opposite wall was a built-in dresser with bookcases built in on either side, all painted white. There were hardwood floors and the woodwork was stained dark. It was the most beautiful room I had ever possessed.

Annie had the third room, in the back, off the kitchen. Annie grew up in the back of beyond, way out past the northern suburbs, in farm country, although her parents were not farmers. Her grandparents were farmers, but her dad sold real estate and also bought real estate, which he subsequently sold or rented. Annie had ten kids in her family, of which she was the oldest. She was a natural beauty with high cheekbones and long, shiny, straight brown hair, and although she was short, she was perfectly proportioned. Linda liked to imply that Annie had no brains whatsoever, and since Annie had never had much opportunity to value her intelligence, she was an easy target.

"She's inane," Linda said. Linda sometimes referred to Annie as "Airhead", which, of course, made Annie very angry. Linda and Annie certainly needed a buffer. Although they worked for the same stockbroker, they had nothing else in common and did not get along very well. As Annie usually got the worst in any encounter, she avoided Linda's company as much as possible, which was fairly easy given that Linda was usually with Peter.

In spite of the subtle hostility between these two I was happy with this new arrangement almost as soon as I moved in. Annie and I got along very well, and Linda, who should have gone to college, respected my degree and my job enough to prevent me from being a target for her sharp tongue.

Annie was a social girl; she still had a number of friends from high school who occasionally came into the city to go out to the bars with her. Annie wanted a husband, and not one from the sticks. She wanted a handsome husband from a good family. She combed the bars every weekend, especially the college bars hoping to meet one.

I was so busy with my first year of school, that at first, I was content to stay at home in the quiet flat to work on lesson plans and mark papers. Luke came to see me a few times, when he could catch a ride, but I was distracted, considering all the problems I was having in the classroom.

Eventually Annie lured me out of the house with her a few Friday and Saturday evenings. She was a 'hit and run' partier. We would go to a bar, park, walk in, get a drink, and walk around, scoping the place out. We would always walk through and around the whole bar. If no one looked interesting by the time our drink was gone we would immediately leave and go to the next bar on the list. If a bar looked promising to Annie, for some unfathomable reason, which I never did decipher, we would settle in. My favorite way to go to a bar is to go with friends, get a table, so I can chat to, and dance with, the friends I came with. Annie never sat down at a table in a bar, although once in a while she perched on a high barstool with her back to the bar. She liked to stand around and wait for a handsome stranger to ask her to dance. Sometimes we met two guy friends who would ask both of us to dance, but often I was left standing by myself. If I didn't want to go, Annie shamed me into it by making me feel like a bad friend, and a social dud. We played out this whole scene weekend after weekend, except when someone had a house party we were invited to. Annie waited all week for the weekends. I tagged along because it was better than staying alone in an empty flat.

Annie met a handsome Southern boy once at a bar. After Annie had been seeing Tad for a while, Tad set up a double date for Annie and him, his college roommate and me. We all met for a few drinks at a bar and ended up at the pool in the park near our apartment, after hours, playing chicken in the dark water with all our clothes on. We were having a very illegal good time until the police kicked us out. They did not give us tickets, just a warning. After changing clothes we went back to their apartment, supposedly to eat. They each went into their bedroom and turned off all the lights, leaving us in the living room with a bowl of popcorn.

I guess we were supposed to follow them into their bedrooms and screw them silly, I was still a virgin, and I was with a guy I didn't even know. I stole an umbrella, since it was raining by then, and Annie and I walked home. They did call to apologize the next day, but I never trusted that Southern boy. Annie thought he was great, and he was charming, but I felt he had a dark side. Even after he stole some jewelry from Linda and a book from me she defended him to the skies. He disappeared and we never saw him again, but Annie brought him up from time to time as her ideal and could never be dissuaded. She insisted that Linda chased him away.

Whenever Annie got a fairly serious boyfriend, Linda would flirt with him and exchange witty, sparkling repartee, until Annie would lose her happy nature and confront Linda. Sometimes Linda slept with the men that Annie liked and ruined the whole relationship. Linda and Peter had an "open" relationship, so she was free to do as she liked. She never met her own men though, she had too much fun stealing Annie's. It was amazing and disturbing to watch someone steal from a beauty by using her wits. And the men seemed quite surprised that in the end they lost both the beauty and the wit.

Of course, my unhappiness and frustration at school spilled over somewhat into my private life, but not as much as you would think. When I got home, I was in my haven and the cares of the day gradually fell away. I would think back over the day and try to analyze what I had done wrong and what I had done right and then I would square my shoulders, vow to do better the next day, and let it all go for a while. A kind of hope would bubble up as I planned lessons or graded papers that the next day would be better and sometimes it was. It took too much energy for my students to be terrible every day.

Then it would be the weekend and Annie would be ready to roll and that would take my mind off the classroom for a while. She was trying to turn me into a social animal. I was her project, along with the soul mate hunting thing. We also went to the park sometimes for a swim or a walk, or went shopping, something we both enjoyed. My first year of teaching I made $6,200 so I wasn't exactly rich, but our whole flat only cost $120, ($40 each) plus utilities. I actually felt quite affluent.

Luke turned eighteen and I guess he decided that it was time to do the deed. It was winter and the flat was cozy and somehow we had it to ourselves. It was probably one of those days in winter break when teachers have a day off, but stockbrokers don't. Of course, I could see the irony of losing my virginity to someone who was only one or two years older than some of my students, but we had been pussyfooting around this huge hunger for a long time. Luke decided that before we "did it", we should get high.

Marijuana had appeared in the flat from time to time, it was still somewhat unusual, but was getting to be more and more common everywhere around the university area. Students smoked joints right outside in the open at concerts.

Luke sat me down in the living room. I remember we had an old green leather couch, large and very comfortable. He set the joints on the coffee table and we lit one up. He took a hit and passed it to me. I shut one eye and took a puff and blew out the smoke.

"You have to inhale," Luke said, my Marlboro man.

So in 1967, the same year the Surgeon General put the first warning on cigarette packs, Luke set out to teach me to inhale. He decided not to waste the marijuana until I got the hang of it.

"Go get your cigarettes," he said. "I'll show you how to inhale a cigarette first."

Now I wanted Luke bad. We had been anticipating the deed since last June. We had the music. We had the incense, we had very little light on that snowy winter day. It looked pretty romantic with the soft brown light filtering through the curtains and the fireplace going. It was now or never.

"OK, here's the cigarettes," I said as I arrived back at the couch from the bedroom. "Now what?"

Luke took out a cigarette for me, lit it, took a drag, and handed it over. I puffed.

"No, you're not inhaling," he said. "There's a little catch in the back of your throat. You have to relax your throat muscles and just let the smoke go down."

I tried that a few times. Nothing.

"Turn around," said Luke. He started to massage my shoulders. As he continues the massage he said, "Now try it."

I tried again and the catch dissolved. The smoke went through and I started to cough. I tried again, no cough. I sat back on the couch and inhaled pensively until I felt a little light-headed.

"Now you're ready," he said.

He lit up the joint once again and sucked the marijuana far down into his lungs and held his breath, his lips in a straight line. After a few minutes he exhaled.

I copied him exactly and after several more coughing fits started to feel what I knew must be a buzz. I felt sort of floaty and light and silly. My brain cells were firing ideas, which spun out and then just disappeared. We started kissing, each kiss deep, seeming to last a long, long time.

"Give me your hand," Luke said, and he pulled me after him into my dark bedroom. He took his time, he undressed me slowly, kissing my neck and mouth. I was opening the snap on his jeans, touching softly whatever was available. After a while there were no more clothes to take off and we moved to the bed. We lay down on tops of the cover. Luke said with some urgency, "Get a towel."

I went naked through the empty apartment and got one of my old towels from the linen closed. It sort of broke the mood though. I spread the towel and dutifully laid myself upon it. We kissed some more. I was warming back up quickly. I was enjoying the wonderful silkiness and completeness of bare skin on bare skin for the first time, something I would never lose a taste for.

Luke moved my hand downwards and gave me his penis. It massaged it and it grew bigger and harder and our breathing grew faster and louder. Then he was on top of me. I liked his weight. He was pausing at the door of me. My body did not seem to want him to gain entrance, but my chemicals did. I pushed towards him and felt the pain and, vaguely, underneath it, the pleasure. I did not experience any heights of ecstasy, but when Luke was finished, he held me close for a while and we slept a bit. Then it was time for him to leave, he had to return the car he borrowed. My roommates would be home soon. He didn't want to see them.

"It'll be better next time," he promised.

I put on a robe and walked him to the door, gave him a kiss and he was gone.

I was finished cleaning my mess and myself before anyone came home. When Linda came in, I was sitting in the corner of the green leather couch with my feet underneath me, tight against my tender privates, inhaling a cigarette and crying. I couldn't stop. The tears just kept coming. Linda came in and sat in the easy chair across from me and asked me if I wanted to talk. I spilled my guts, of course, and she was actually very sympathetic and understanding. She said it was like that for her the first time.

"He didn't hurt you did he?" she asked.

"No more than he had to," I said, "I don't know why I'm crying," I said.

"It's just that after he left I felt so sad."

"Let me change my clothes," Linda said, "You go wash your face and put on some makeup. We'll go out and celebrate your first time."

"Where's Annie," I asked.

"She had to work overtime," Linda answered.

We went to the best Chinese restaurant and soon the table was covered with footed stainless steel dishes with silvery covers. Linda told me all about her first sexual encounter, which happened to her at a much younger age than mine had. She had fallen for a painter, much older than her, who lived an unconventional life in an old church in her hometown. After that first experience they had quite a long affair, which ended badly. She was so nice to me that my heart started to warm to her a bit, without forgetting some of her transgressions against Annie. By the time we left (we also had a couple of drinks) I felt much more festive and ready to get back to planning for Christmas with my family and at the apartment, and to planning lessons for the new semester. I decided I would not think about the reality of school, just the logistics. I didn't want to begin to dread going back until I absolutely had to.

So I lost two maidenheads in one day, one in my throat, and one, you know where. From that day on I have never stopped inhaling tobacco smoke. It became a terrible addiction for me. I lost my psychological equanimity without my nicotine. And some of you will think I became a sex addict too, although I don't really know about that. Fortunately, although marijuana became a fixture in my life for a while, I was never addicted to it. This combination of sex and cigarettes was enough to bring about my ultimate downfall though, and addicted or not, the drugs played a part too.

Chapter 14

Hobart

Hobart looked like James Dean in the pictures we had of him as a young man. Family lore has it that he marched to his own drummer. He didn't like drinking, smoking, swearing, or womanizing. He was not religious, just had very high moral standards for himself and for everyone around him. He was actually a loner, who always longed to be by himself. His dream life was to be a hermit in a shack full of books. He loved to fish, and had obviously spent time hunting, although he never was really fond of hunting. He loved mechanical things; especially cars, and he always had a car, starting with a Model A. He also owned a few trucks over the years. As far as I know he never owned a new car in his life and the best car he ever drove was a luxury rental that he drove once. On that particular occasion it was the only model available when he and mom were driving home from Florida. He was into late middle age by then.

Although Hobart wanted to be alone, he rarely was. He was actually quite popular and had a close circle of friends and relatives that he apparently drove to picnics, parties, beaches, and various other low cost events. My mom hung out with Hobart and his crew for six years before they married.

Hobart had to drop out of school in the eighth grade. His parents were not able to find work. It was the depression. His first job involved making deliveries on roller skates, a messenger service. In his late twenties he opened a garage and gas station with one of his good friends. The garage was forced out of business when his partner absconded with the funds. There was a great deal of bitterness about this and their friendship never recovered. After that, Hobart, not married, went to work in factories. When World War II broke out he was not accepted in the armed forces for several reasons, one of which involved being the sole support of his parents and later because he was in an "essential war industry" which he never described to us.

I cannot imagine my father as a soldier. He was a solitary man in his heart and soul, with none of that locker room camaraderie which seems to help men survive in such environments. I suppose no one can really picture her or his father jumping out of a foxhole with a blazing gun or riding on a tank or marching in mud, or running off a U-boat into a brutal rain of machine gun fire. The fact that he did not participate in the war as a soldier cut him off further from his peers. No Veterans of Foreign Wars for Dad, no old war buddies stopping by the house. The neighborhood men in Smithvale who were his peers had all fought in the war. He was suspect to them and he lost an "in" in the good old boy network that might have helped him have greater career success. He never acted as if this bothered him at all.

When he was not working he could be found outside doing something "around the house". There was always yard work to do and repairs to the house, and cars to keep on the road. The cellar was his domain also. His workshop was on the opposite side of the cellar from the washing machine and was well equipped with hammers, screwdrivers, drills and saws; jars of nuts and bolts, tacks and nails, all organized along a shelf behind the workbench. Little boxes with tiny drawers held every small piece of hardware that might ever be of use. There were various motors and car parts scattered over the workbench waiting to be rebuilt or to be plugged in to the latest used car. Later there were shoeboxes full of vacuum tubes to repair TV's and radios for extra cash.

Hobart was the kind of dad who made you feel that he would take care of his family, no matter what it took. He was also a judgmental dad who led by example. He ruled by disapproval and disappointment. He disapproved of drinking, smoking, lying, tattling, gossiping whining, and refusing to pull your weight. He had honed disappointment to a fine weapon. The worst thing any of his children or even his wife could do was to not live up to his high expectation. We all hated to disappoint Dad because his disapproval was expressed in silence, a silence that had a weight. He would seem crushed by the weakness of your character and you would have to atone for your behavior before the weight of his silence would lift.

It was a traditional household in many ways. There were girls' chores and boy's chores. Boys' chores involved taking out the garbage and doing yard work with Dad. Girls' chores included ironing, setting the table, picking up, watching younger siblings, and most dreaded of all, doing the dishes. We girls felt, to begin with, that the division of chores was unfair and of course they were, but this argument held no sway. We assigned ourselves turns at table setting and dish washing and drying.

Although we had six girls for many years only three of us were old enough to do the dishes, Felicity, Gertie, and me. Our family made a mountain of dishes. Every evening after dinner there were dishes all over the kitchen. Often we would get right to it, but there were always nights when we procrastinated, got interested in a program on TV, started reading a book, started a board game. If we waited just a little too long, Dad would snap. Then he would go out in the kitchen and do the dishes, his lips in a tight line. Then you were not allowed to jump in and help. You were banished from the kitchen and you slunk away to sulk in some corner of the house. Your banishment from parental favor would continue until the next day when you would usually, of your own free will, pitch in and complete some self-assigned chore to get back in Dad's good graces. Even Mom would occasionally earn the silent treatment.

If Mom was the heart of our family, Dad was its conscience. He did not believe in holding others to a standard to which one did not hold one's self. He also believed "actions speak louder than words.' Although when we were young he sometimes had a "cocktail" or a "high ball", by the time we were teenagers he did not drink at all and made it clear that he was disappointed if we did. Maybe he lucked out and missed out on that alcohol addiction gene which the rest of his family seemed to have inherited in spades, but it was clear that he exercised self-discipline.

I never heard my father swear. Hobart's worst curse was "Jesus H. Christ", which made me nervous for his "immortal soul". I learned about our "immortal soul" on the school bus. Every day I sat with a good Catholic girl, Mary Margaret. Mary Margaret helped me lament the fact that I wasn't born Catholic. She told me that even if I converted, the best I could hope for was purgatory. I didn't really buy into this as it seemed way less advantageous than my own religion in which going straight to heaven was a distinct possibility, but I did get attached to the idea of an "immortal soul." Hobart never picked up a cigarette while he was my father, and he never mentioned whether he tried one as a young man. Dad's father used to visit us on Sunday's when we still lived in the city. He was a short, rotund Frenchman who wore a dark suit and tie and smoked big smelly cigars. He died when I was five. No one blamed his death on the cigars.

I don't think my brother's drinking or my smoking was a rebellious act against an inflexible parent. Although we did these things, it was always with the awareness of Hobart's deep disappointment. His disappointment became ours, because, even though we did these things, we lost respect for ourselves as we did them. Just to drink or smoke proved that we were lacking in self-discipline.

Hobart had trouble dealing with a houseful of teen-aged daughters. He was extremely modest. We never saw either of our parents unclothed except in bathing suits or, rarely, pajamas. He not only had a houseful of teenage girls, but also, usually a houseful of teenage boys who were not family. He was adamant that we not appear downstairs until we were fully clothed. Gertie was the only daughter who did not take to modesty. She was the girl in the family who learned to change her entire outfit in the car, without showing anything at all. She was the sister who taught us how to remove our bra without taking off our shirt or blouse. She wouldn't have minded changing in the middle of the living room. She taught herself the clandestine undressing techniques out of respect for Dad.

When Dad was in a light-hearted mood, he could be quite cheerful and fun. Sometimes when we did the dishes without argument or delay he would join us and treat us to a display of terrible yodeling until we were begging him to leave the kitchen. Or he would treat us to a chorus of "I have tears in my ears from lying on my back in my bed while I cried over you." In a good mood he would give us lessons in how to turn a light switch on and off with a dishtowel. Most of us can probably still perform this amazing feat. We spent a lot of time trying to keep Dad cheerful, but we were young and selfish and many an evening went by without a yodel.

Hobart was also our hero, sometimes a very awkward one, but he hated to see his children hurt or unhappy. Once we stopped to get ice cream cones at an ice cream stand on the main road through Smithvale. I got to ride "shotgun", a privilege I never usually won. I leaned against my door as we pulled out onto the highway and fell right out on the road. My father's reflexes were so swift, that he stopped the car, jumped out and stopped traffic before I even started crying. After he comforted me, with his adrenalin levels probably through the roof, he took me back around and got me another ice cream, this time making sure my door was locked.

When I was living in the apartment by the park I had a very bad day, a day when I could not stop crying – probably PMS, although we did not have that term. Hobart appeared at my door, probably sent by Augusta. It was clear that he had no idea what to do but he had aspirin for me to take, and a few food delicacies that he picked up at the market. He made me take the aspirin right away and then give him a tour of the apartment. I was very touched by his gauche thoughtfulness and he did chase my blues away.

Luke said that I overlooked my father's flaws. He said that, for one thing, we didn't have to be so poor. He said that my dad could have been a foreman at the shop, but he could not force himself to go against his nature or his own wishes, even for the sake of his family's finances. I remember that this had been a tough decision for my father. He took his position as a union steward very seriously and felt by becoming a management employee he would be betraying his fellow union members. I'm not sure how Luke got his information; probably he had talked about it with Robert. Anyway, Luke insisted that Hobart should have made this sacrifice for his family. It was certainly an interesting new take on my father, but I really didn't agree. My father's strict personal values were important to me.

I could, of course, go on and on about Hobart, who couldn't write a whole book about their father, but I'm almost done for now. Hobart's one other outstanding trait was his very fine brain. He was smart. He understood electronics intuitively and could have been an engineer if born into other circumstances. The house in Smithvale had antique wiring. Anytime we wanted to add a modern appliance Hobart had to go down into the cellar and perform some electrical magic.

Eventually he reached the limits of the current wiring arrangement. When the wringer washer gave way to an electric washer and dryer and a new electric range was added to the kitchen, a 220 circuit had to be added. Hobart drew his plans, bought his supplies, and rewired the house adding a brand new electrical box. It had to be inspected by some official agency after it was installed. They tried to give Hobart a hard time but it was correctly done and they ultimately had to approve it.

He took a home course in calculus, when he needed it to qualify for a job off the main line at work, and he passed it easily. He spent many a night with all of us around the dining room table before he worked nights, helping us with our homework. He made it clear to all of us that education had a high priority in his view. Everyone in or family finished high school and five of us completed at least two years of higher education. Robert and his friends christened him with the nickname "Brain."

Chapter 15

1968

It was the summer of 1968. I was done with teaching for now and out looking for a job. I found one almost immediately at the university in the Psych. Department. They had a federal grant to study Head Start programs around the state to see if preschools were an effective use of government funds. I was impressed. I did not realize that our government exercised such detailed oversight. I thought they just saw a problem, threw some money at it, and let the chips fall where they may, until they took the money away and threw it at some new problem. But, anyway, not the case with Head Start. Apparently twelve different universities scattered around the nation where conducting a variety of studies. All of the projects were set up to test all Head Start students at randomly selected centers both pre-program and post program.

I worked from a little office, on the other side of the same park where I lived, with some very interesting characters. Our secretary, Jackie Jarvis, was from Jamaica. She could speak the "patois" of the island. She was exotic and, at times, raunchy. Our boss, Jon, was blond, Scandinavian, gorgeous, and from a wealthy family. I was a tester and a coder. Reenie, the other tester was a thin blonde dying to be in love with our Jonnie.

The three of us would be scheduled out of the office traveling several days per week and in the office coding the days when we weren't traveling. Most of our traveling was done as day trips. At one center we did have to stay in a hotel for a week at a time. This was a busy job and a great job. Of course, four-year-olds are not very verbal, so IQ questions were pretty basic. Introduce subject to cow, show picture, say - "This is a cow." Show next page with cow mixed in with other animals. Ask, "Can you find the cow?" Head Start children were often even less verbal than a typical four-year-old as Head Start looked for children who were "disadvantaged" in some way (often in several ways). Some of our urban kids had never before seen or heard of a cow. The rural kids had. It made a difference, but even so you could see that the tests revealed information about cognitive content and process. Other tests asked basic questions –

What is your first name? – What is your last name? – Point to red. – Point to the circle. – Who is your best friend in school? Every child in our sample schools was tested.

Jon, Jackie, Reenie, and I loved our jobs. We felt the task was relevant and the job was not difficult. We were all so light-hearted together, laughed so much and smoked so many cigarettes. You could smoke cigarettes almost anywhere in those days, except in the Head Start centers. You could smoke in offices, in restaurants, in cars, in homes, at outdoor rock concerts, in hotels, in airplanes. Reenie and I smoked up a storm riding to the various centers while she pined over Jon, who, if we were to believe Jackie, was not interested in women.

 Reenie refused to believe it. So we would smoke and Reenie would yearn as we criss-crossed the state testing four-year-olds. We also had to have a year-long study. We chose the area of "positive" and "negative reinforcement" or "praise" and "blame". We would quantify the amount and type of "praise" or "blame" given to each subject on a grid, code our findings in FORTRAN and forward them to the federal government.

Every Friday we would rest in the office and Jackie and Jonnie would start. It always began the same way. "Jonnie, my left tit itches," Jackie would say, in her lilting island way. And they would be off, on a perfectly safe but exceedingly hot sexual riff while Reenie and I listened, at first shocked silly, eventually used to it, happily entertained.

Although I was busy during the week I was still available to go barhopping with Annie on weekends. Sometimes Reenie came along. Luke still showed up from time to time with some pot that we were all happy to smoke. We'd get the album cover and the papers and the rolling lessons would begin. Rolling a good joint took time and concentration especially if it wasn't the first one of the evening, if the music, maybe a Beatles album, was sucking you in and out like a tide and everyone was mellow and hungry. Small, tight, and uniform were the qualities you were judged on. As the "j" passed from person to person, as breaths were held all around the circle, the "j" could not fall apart enroute and had to last down to the hot rolled paper at the end when only a roach clip would safely hold it. Sometimes there was hashish in a small pipe or a hookah or a bong. People dropped by, time flew away like bubbles- oh, look at that – pop – gone – where'd it go, next bubble – oh-h-h.

We started out conservatively, me in my little teacher clothes, the stockbrokers in their office clothes. Annie and I continued making the rounds of the bars, admittedly sometimes setting off slightly stoned. But my new job did not require formal attire and we were living near a big university. Everyone was getting "hippified", groovin', with long swingy hair on boys and girls, afros everywhere, dreads. Gradually we put aside our mini dresses and our skirts and blouses. We shopped at the army-navy stores – painter jeans (both the cream and the blue), and work boots – at the import store – embroidered tops from Mexico and India. We wore beaded or macramé bracelets and sometimes headbands. Annie left her job working with the stockbroker. She took a job in retail. She was not so into the pot scene but liked being stylish so she looked the hippie part.

Summer was the best time to be a hippie because what was happening was a group phenomenon and people liked to parade around the university area with other "freaks", or sit on a sunny hill, across from the main university business district, with very little grass, dubbed "the beach". We attended outdoor concerts all that summer where joints were passed through the crowd. "Give peace a chance." It was a huge love fest. We felt that we were all one consciousness, one mind, and one heart. Since the communication was mostly nonverbal except for whatever music we were listening to, and a few polite "man, want a hits" accompanied by an arm tapping yours with a joint held out for you, it was easy to be in sync. We all did our weekly work, but it wasn't what our life was about. "We can change the world, rearrange the world."

Lena came by our place with a kilo of grass. That was a lot of grass. Grass usually came in nickel or dime bags, which after you picked out all the twigs and seeds, had to be used sparingly. We knew grass was illegal so we did hide it. We also knew how to act straight even though we were stoned "out of our gourds." But it didn't feel all that illegal. Everyone smoked right out in the open. In the neighborhoods where we lived people smoked pot in cars, even at indoor concerts. Rarely was anyone arrested unless they were belligerent or rowdy. We called the cops "pigs," but they usually showed remarkable restraint where we were concerned. I only realized how different the rest of the world was when I went home to Smithvale on Sundays. At first it was easy to blend my two world, but as I became more of a "stoner" it was much more bizarre to go home.

So Lena brought the kilo to our apartment and we all helped clean and weigh and package it. With her New York City connections she had decided to go into business. We got so high just breathing and handling the marijuana, not smoking it, just taking it in through our pores, a magnificent "contact high," that we gave no thought at all to the legality, morality or anything but the pleasure of the music pounding around us, and the conversation, however repetitive and evanescent, and the high.

Sometimes there were parties with outsiders. Linda knew a lot of people. Annie always had some cutie hovering around. But I liked it best when it was just "family," especially with Linda trying to steal all Annie's men. I found I did not like conflict. I was a peacemaker. I wanted life to flow along happily from day to day without personal stress. Where there are people, there is always conflict, which even I, with all my talent and energy, could not defuse.

By the summer of 1969 we were many tokes away from the summer of 1968. Life was very, very good. Even news from the world outside reached us only intermittently. The fact that campus strikes could and did become violent registered. Black Power registered. The assassination of Dr. Martin Luther King made a huge impression. But our revolution was nonviolent. It was all peace and love. We were aglow with the wonder of "grass" roots, evolutionary change, at least some of us were. When Bobbie Kennedy was assassinated sadness and fear rocked paradise, but paradise steadied again and "Reefer Madness" ruled the day. "Don't bogart that joint."

Chapter 16

With the Taylors

Sundays were spent back in Smithvale with my real family. It took only fifteen minutes to get there but all day to get back in the rhythm of the family. Life at the Taylor household went on much as it always had with a few changes. Felicity was married so she no longer lived at home, Tyler was in Vietnam, and Gertie was a new bride. Only four of the eight Taylors were living at home.

We seemed to be split into two families, the grown ups and the kids. Robert, Emily, Rebecca, and Morgan were still home, past the Robert torture days, into the "In-a-Gadda-da-Vida" days. The revolution hit the younger four somewhat, the older three not at all. Robert had mutton chop sideburns and wore his hair longer; the girls wore flowered mini skirts and dresses with white go-go boots. Their hair was long and straight and their pant legs were wider. The styles in public schools were changing.

My family welcomed me, but they were withholding judgment. I still had a good job, I was evolving slowly, but I fit in less each time I visited. Even so Sundays unfolded as tradition demanded. We sat around the living room and chatted. We watched Felicity's new baby, took turns holding and feeding the baby, we laughed and ate and celebrated being Taylors.

Our family was actually larger because Felicity came with Dean and the baby, Abby, Gertie and Jason came with their puppy, Waffles, and Tyler's pregnant wife, Sara was usually with us, Tyler being always on our minds and in our conversation.

Augusta would cook Sunday dinner and then all of us "girls" would help: peel the potatoes, cut up the vegetables, set the table, scrub the pots and pans. We no longer fit at the table and often had to eat buffet style. In summer we always ate outside on picnic tables, weather permitting, and sat around the semi-bare backyard in lawn chairs. Hobart's grass was slowly coming back as backyard games died out.

In the summer of '68 Hobart had to deal with a cement block cellar wall that was buckling. He was grateful to have new male energy in the family, and although he missed Tyler, Dean and Jason helped fill the void. They also helped with the cellar wall project. First they had to install jack posts in the basement to hold the house up while the wall was removed. Then they had to dig out the offending cellar wall to expose and remove the old cement blocks. Most could be reused with new mortar. They had to rebuild the wall, fill in along the outside and lower the house slowly back onto the new wall. This was a huge project and a hungry one, so lots of cooking was also required.

I kept going home, almost every Sunday, even though I had to wiggle my way back into the family each time, even though it became clear that my family approved less and less of my lifestyle. I helped with the cooking, sat around and talked, talked, talked, did dishes, set tables, and held Abby whenever it was my turn. I found my family hopelessly conservative and square, no revolution happening here, which should have been a clue that the cultural impact of the hippie movement was not quite as widespread as I imagined. I refused, however, to believe that my family reflected the American majority more closely than I did. I loved them, but felt that I was in the mainstream and they were in a little backwater somewhere. Felicity was still styling herself on Jackie Kennedy Onassis for heaven's sake. Who's judging whom?

Once in a while Annie came with me to visit my family or I went with her to visit her family. Annie's family lived out in the sticks. She was the oldest in a family with ten kids. Most of her sisters and brothers were quite young. They thought we were as cool as we thought we were. At Annie's house we played baseball with the kids or sat in the crowded kitchen and talked with her mom, Wilma. Her Dad, Harwin, would bustle in from his travels, order Wilma to find some papers he needed for one of his real estate deals and then disappear again.

I think Annie's family had more money, but less available cash than mine. Annie also had a brother who was born hydrocephalic and irreversibly brain damaged. He was treated like any other member of the family, dressed each morning and carried downstairs, but he could not sit up, could not feed himself, and would always wear diapers. Everyone lived his or her life around him, and all the care of him fell to Wilma, who fortunately was a cheerful and sassy soul. His disability affected every aspect of Annie's family's life. Annie took very few people home with her. She loved her family but her desire to escape was palpable. We didn't go there often.

On Mondays, in our pretty apartment by the park, we would wake up to our jobs and our music and our friends, our movies, our concerts, our barhopping and our increasingly more frequent highs. We felt more at home with this life than we did with our own families.

Chapter 17

USA, 1969

In 1969 the five most watched TV shows were: Rowan and Martin's Laugh-In, Gomer Pyle MSMC, Bonanza, Mayberry RFD, and Family Affair. A half-gallon of milk cost 55¢, gas/gallon, 35¢, one pound of butter, 85¢, one loaf of white bread, 23¢. The minimum wage was $1.60.

Movies we watched in 1969 included: Sweet Charity, Funny Girl, Midnight Cowboy, True Grit, Take the Money and Run, Goodbye Columbus, Alice's Restaurant, Butch Cassidy and the Sundance Kid, Oh What a Lovely War, Bob and Carol and Ted and Alice, The Sterile Cuckoo, Goodbye Mr. Chips, and They Shoot Horses Don't They.

Slaughterhouse Five, The Love Machine, The French Lieutenant's Woman, and Portnoy's Complaint were all on the New York Times Bestseller's Lists.

Everywhere everyday life reflected the split between the "counter culture" and the "mainstream" culture. At least it did to me. Even the news seemed split between the two camps.

The "counter culture" news went like this. The Two Virgins album released by John and Yoko was banned from stores as pornographic. Early in the year Heard it Through the Grapevine by Marvin Gaye was the #1 hit. The Beatles made their last ever appearance as a group performing on the roof of Apple Studios. The Smothers Brothers Comedy Hour was cancelled for political reasons when they had Joan Baez as a guest. Jim Morrison of the Doors was arrested for allegedly exposing himself during a show. Biafra threatened to become "one of the great catastrophes of modern times." The Chicago 8 were indicted after disturbances and demonstrations at the

Democratic National Convention. Paul McCartney married Linda Eastman. In April Aquarius (Let the Sun Shine In) by the 5th Dimension was the #1 single, followed by Get Back by the Beatles. The #1 album was Blood, Sweat and Tears. Police removed a group from People's Park near the Berkeley Campus causing one death. Dr. Timothy Leary was convicted and sentenced to 5-30 years for bringing marijuana from Mexico to Texas and failing to pay taxes on it. John and Yoko held a Bed Love-In in Toronto for world peace, harmony and love throughout the world.

In May the #1 album was Hair. Rolling Stone guitarist Brian Jones was found dead from accidental drowning with high blood levels of alcohol and barbiturates. In August Charles Manson and his followers committed bloody murder. The Woodstock Nation convened. In the fall the #1 single was Honky Tonk Woman by the Rolling Stones and the #1 album was Blind Faith by Blind Faith. Bob Dylan changes his sound and is backed by the Band. Monty Python's Flying Circus airs in the US for the first time.

October 15th is Moratorium on War Day with huge marches in major cities. Rumors say that "Paul is Dead." The #1 single is I Can't Get Close to You by the Temptations and after that Green River by Creadance Clearwater Revival. Jim Morrison is arrested for public drunkenness on a flight although the charges are dropped. The #1 album by November is Abbey Road by the Beatles. There is a huge Washington War Protest on November 16th. On December 6th the Rolling Stones are at Altamont Speedway. They allow the Hell's Angels to act as bodyguards. One fan is killed when he rushes the stage, others are injured. 89 Native Americans occupy Alcatraz. They want funding for cultural centers among other things. A Gallup poll in December results in the statement that 22% of college students have tried marijuana. Tiny Tim and Alice are married on the Johnnie Carson Show.

The more "mainstream" events of 1969 also reflect an era of deep change. In January, THE FTC PROPOSES TO BAN CIGARETTE ADS ON TV AND RADIO STATING THAT CIGARETTE

SMOKING POSES A SERIOUS DANGER TO PUBLIC
HEALTH. Lyndon B. Johnson bids farewell to Congress. Jack
Griffith at Cal Tech first photographs the DNA double helix through
an electron microscope.

The trial of accused assassin of Robert Kennedy, Sirhan Sirhan,
begins in LA. Throughout the year planes are hijacked to Cuba.
Richard Nixon is inaugurated. The #1 single is Crimson and Clover
by Tommy James and the Shondells. James Earl Ray pleads guilty to
the assassination of Martin Luther King and is sentenced to 99 years
in prison. At the Grammies, Best Record goes to Mrs. Robinson,
while best album goes to By the Time I Get to Phoenix. In late
spring Sirhan Sirhan is convicted to death in the gas chamber.

In May one of the bloodiest battles in Vietnam occurs, the "Battle of
Hamburger Hill." The FBI discloses that it authorized wiretaps of
Martin Luther King right up to the time of his death. In June a
rubella vaccine becomes available. Charles Evers is elected the first
ever Black major of a biracial city. The #1 song is In the Year 2525
by Zager and Evans. Ted Kennedy drives off a bridge in Martha's
Vineyard at Chappaquiddick Island with Mary Jo Kopechne. She dies
and he fails to report the incident for ten hours. On July 30th Neil
Armstrong is the first man to walk on the moon. He utters the
famous words, "The Eagle has Landed." Jackie Onasis celebrates her
40th birthday. Hurricane Camille hits the Gulf Coast leaving 320
dead. MacDonald's introduces the Big Mac. Ho Chi Minh dies at 79.

The first stage reduction of troops in Vietnam is completed in
August. The #1 song is Sugar, Sugar by the Archies. Marcus Welby,
MD and The Brady Bunch premiere on TV. A report is released
which states that violence on TV leads to real life violence. 140,000
GE workers go on strike. The #1 song is October is Suspicious
Minds by Elvis Presley. A Supreme Court decision says segregation in
schools must end at once. Maxi skirts are shown. The President
announces complete withdrawal of all troops but does not disclose a
schedule for withdrawal. Sesame Street premieres.

In the fall the #1 song is Wedding Bell Blues by the 5th Dimension, the #1 album is Abbey Road by the Beatles. In November Wendy's opens. By December 60,000 more troops have been pulled out of Vietnam.

Chapter 18

My 1969

My boss decided to leave the Head Start grant project. He appointed me his heir apparent so I was expecting a promotion and a substantial raise. On the strength of these expectations I bought a new car, a sports car, an Austin Healey Sprite. It looked cute but was really a cheap piece of shit (yes, my language was evolving). It crumpled like a tin can if anything so much as touch it. The front end was dented almost as soon as I registered it. Jonnie was driving and did not notice that the car in front had stopped. I shrugged it off, but did not report it to my insurance. It wasn't too bad. Rich boy Jonnie did not offer to pay.

My promotion never materialized. The federal government decided not to renew four of the university grants. Our grant was one of the four. Apparently our praise/blame study did not wow them. Not only was I not promoted: I was once again unemployed. With a brand new car (which only someone raised in poverty would have purchased in the first place)! Ineligible for unemployment payment, federal grants being year-to-year contracts! Quelle panic! I just did not know what to do. Without work I was free to smoke cigarettes all day, ashtrays full of butts, cigarettes barely within my budget as I had some savings.

Looking for a job was definitely in order, but the job search was not going as well this time. I typed an updated resume and hauled out the old teacher clothes, but my new curly afro-style hair was not impressing employers. And I probably smelled like patchouli. Annie, since she worked retail, was often home days. She worked crazy retail hours. She wanted to go, to do, to hang out. In July we went to Newport to the jazz festival. This festival usually concentrated on classic jazz, but in 1969 they invited people like James Brown and Led Zeppelin, The town had no idea what they were in for. Annie had a black Malibu convertible that she loved. We set off one sunny July day. In Massachusetts we picked up two young hitchhikers who ended up being from the same street we lived on. This is the way things went in the 60's.

We had no tickets to any of the events, and could not devise a way to get inside the fences. Sometimes we hung out near the fences to listen and watch through the links, but usually we wandered around town, or along the sea wall by the Newport "summer homes" (mansions), or at the beach.

So many people came that the town was overrun. Gas station owners parked cars in front of the rest rooms so that no one could get in. Restaurants put up signs, "no shirt, no shoes, no service" or "you cannot use the rest rooms unless you are a patron." We, fortunately, met some people who let us use their motel bathroom for a small fee, but physically we were slightly dirtier and a lot less comfortable than usual.

The group we really wanted to see was Led Zeppelin. Late Sunday it was rumored that they were not coming. The rumor spread like wildfire. Someone told Annie that this was not true. They actually were coming. Everyone started to leave but Annie would not go. We inherited some tickets from people who were convinced the group would not appear. We entered the concert grounds for the first time and saw Paul Winter Group and B.B King. Around midnight, when the crowd had gotten pretty sparse, Led Zeppelin arrived. It was electric. We all stood on our chairs and rocked out. We left for home about 3 am. Annie was vindicated. I would never be allowed to forget this.

In August we went to Woodstock. We packed up the Austin Healey, clothing, food, borrowed tents, sleeping bags, and headed down the New York State Thruway to Yasgur's farm with about 250,000 other people, another quarter of a million having already arrived there.

We weren't allowed to get anywhere near the farm, had to park the Austin Healey along the side of a country road with cars lining the verges as far as the eye could see. You had to walk from there. We left everything locked in the car except my cigarettes and joined the freak parade. Oh, it was wonderful! All around us a whole hippie nation, young, in "high" spirits, each one more hip than the last, music pouring from speakers rigged to telephone poles, a sunny summer day.

Part of something so huge, so much to see, gorgeous long-haired guys, no shirts, dirty blue jeans, sandals. Long-haired women all rigged out in long flowy dresses and beads and sandals, jeans and Mexican wedding shirts-headbands, arm in arm. Joints were passed, jugs of wine were shared, tabs of acid were dropped. It was better than any New York City Easter Parade, better than the Ascot races, a parade of a new world set to a rock beat. Jimi Hendrix's version of "The Star Spangled Banner." Bad things were rumored, but we did not see anything scary. We were peaking. The whole world was peaking.

We had walked for about an hour when cars started to come through again. Apparently the flood overcame the ability of the police to control it. We ended up riding on the roof of a station wagon, full inside, with more people on the tailgate. The sun went down on our new age caravan and eventually we climbed down and spent the night at a campsite in the woods with friendly strangers. A slice of bread handed to us by a compassionate soul was all we had to eat.

When we woke up it was raining. Started out as showers, soon a downpour settled in for the long haul. We had no umbrellas, were water soaked, our hair draggled around our faces, as was everyone's. People still trying to be playful, but with slippery clay mud everywhere it go messy. Lit a cigarette, it turned soggy and broke apart after a few puffs. The road was the only place you could actually walk without sliding so we set out to walk back to the car far away down the country road. Annie had to go to work on Monday. The rain stopped, we dried out, but it remained overcast. Now two lanes of people, those walking out and those still walking in. Still a grand and interesting passage with everyone eyeballing everyone else and the music again from the speakers. Finally, the car, a quick snack and home, back to my unemployed reality.

Chapter 19
Jane Austen in the Park

I felt so free. Women were still in arranged marriages, having their feet bound, and in other male-dominated situations all around the world, but not in America. We were equals with our men. We had the pill. Surprise babies were a thing of the past. We could smoke cigarettes, go to college, have jobs. We could go wherever we wanted to go and do whatever we wanted to do. What a privileged time in which to be born. We could wear jeans and sit cross-legged on the ground and get high and read books all day, and eat out in restaurants whenever we could afford to. We did not need our father's brother's, uncle's, boyfriend's, husband's permission to do any of these things.

What would Jane Austen think? I picture the clothes she had to wear, the socially orchestrated life she had to live.

I'm in the park by the rose garden sitting on the brick stairs at the end of the brick walk, just enjoying the warm sunniness of the day and the smell of cut grass and roses. I'm wearing an embroidered Indian white on white top of lightweight cotton and my khaki carpenter jeans with the little loop for a hammer. My white Dr. Scholl's sandals are thrust out in front of me. I'm resting on my elbows, catching a few rays.

I turn and open my eyes and I see Jane Austen walking towards me down the garden path drenched in dappled summer sun and shadows filtered through the old maples and oaks that line the path. She doesn't see me yet. She seems to float down the brick walk in her long skirted dress, head high, back perfectly straight. She has slipper-type shoes with low heels. They are off-white with a bow on the front. Her dress is in the Greek style, empire waist, skirts flowing softly to the tips of her shoes. It looks like an everyday dress, cream background, small floral design, maybe roses, in pinks and greens, perhaps a chintz. The dress has a V-neck with a wide creamy cotton collar, spotless, and sleeves just above the elbow with a crisp creamy lace edge. She has the handles of a woven handbag twined around her gloved right hand. It's one of those small pouch-type bags, pulling on the handles closes the top of the bag. Her hair is brown, piled atop her head, no loose ends. She has a summer straw picture hat on her head, pink and green ribbons around the brim, trailing down her back. A puzzled expression crosses her delicate features. She doesn't recognize her surroundings.

She sees me and her puzzlement increases momentarily before she takes control of her expression. In spite of her control, I can see that she is scandalized. I remember I am braless. Perhaps, though, that is the least conspicuous of my transgressions.

"Good morning, Ms. Austen," I say.

"Where am I she says?" forgetting her usually excellent manners.

"You're not really here," I say, "You're just a figment of my imagination."

"Oh, thank goodness. I was somewhere that made me very happy," she says, "I wouldn't want to get lost."

"Where were you? Was it heaven? What was it like?" I ask.

"Oh we're not allowed to talk about that," she says.

"Please sit down. Sit down here on the steps with me." I say, moving down a few steps to make room for her big dress. Maybe we could have a conversation."

She is not overly fastidious. She sinks gracefully to perch on the top step. She looks me over.

"My dear," she says, "What are you wearing? I have never seen such clothing. Pants on a women! Where are your undergarments?"

"Call me Zoe, Ms. Austen", I say, "This is the year 1969, and my friends all dress like this. We're members of a large social movement called 'hippies'."

"1969?" she repeated astounded, "America? Hippies?"

Her eyes started to glaze over.

"We have a commercial for cigarettes that says 'You've come a long way, baby.' We are also in the middle of a social revolution called the "Women's Liberation Movement'," I say, "I got you here to see what you think of our new freedoms."

"Cigarettes? Commercial? Baby?" she echoes, still not focusing as I would have liked.

"Cigarettes are tobacco rolled in paper," I tell her, "a commercial is an advertisement and, since women can smoke cigarettes openly now and they once could not the ad is speaking to women. Baby is modern slang, used to show how cool and hip women are now."

"Cool?" she says, "Hip?"

"Never mind," I say, I really just wanted you to notice how free we are. We have a pill. If we take it every day we don't get pregnant. We can have as many lovers or as much sexual intercourse as we like because we are protected as long as we remember to take that pill. We don't have to wear skirts all the time and we don't need the protection of a man. We can come and go as we like, even have an education and a career."

She thinks, taking in all I have said.

"My dear Zoe," she says, "You are not as free as you imagine. Given the nature of some men, who can be as evil as the Devil, I think you will find that total freedom for women is a myth. And while the idea of an education for women is wondrously marvelous, and even having projects that occupy the mind is a concept I can grasp, a woman's reputation will always be important and must be guarded at all times. Women, like men, will never be totally free. Free to do what? To be low and depraved. Sexuality, free of love is an abomination leading to the basest kinds of behavior."

I didn't argue, although this encounter had not gone quite as I expected. Apparently Jane did not envy my freedom as much as I had hoped she would. I just gave myself a knowing little "I know better" smile and made my politest good-byes. I was satisfied with the contrast between our situations, certain that I was infinitely more sophisticated and that modern women should have knocked the socks off of Ms. Jane Austen. All of her warnings were just anachronistic (excuse me) "bullshit". (She would have frowned over that vulgarism, but, to underline my point, I was free to say it.)

I stood up, took one last whiff of the roses and walked home, by myself.

Chapter 20

With the Taylors Again

Tyler came home from Vietnam in 1969 because his twins were born quite premature and very tiny. Two little boys fighting to breathe while their lungs developed. They weighed two something and one something and we started to believe that they would live. Tyler, who had spent his time in Vietnam in the motor pool thanks to the many hours spent with Hobart with his head under a car hood, was released on a hardship discharge. Even though he was not a combat troop, he had seen enough to last a lifetime and did not want to talk about it. The winter was spent visiting the hospital and waiting for the twins to add weight. Sara, always an anxious woman, held up remarkably well once Tyler got home. One twin was a great concern to the doctors; they were quite negative about his chances.

This was the first Taylor family crisis in which life and death of an infant was involved. My mom and dad had friends whose young daughter was killed in a farm accident and our favorite aunt died of kidney disease. But these guys were babies and they were Tyler's babies. The Taylors rallied to help Tyler and Sara by lavishing lots of home cooking, love, and attention on them.

By summer the twins were both home and doing very well. They were curly blonds like Tyler had been and their intelligence was already obvious. Tyler and Sara bought a mobile home and some land out in the same sticks where Annie's family lived.

Gertie and Jason also had a boy, also curly blond hair, but much chubbier – a very smiley social butterfly who had charmed his way into all our hearts. I was the only one of the first four without a husband and a child and Augusta was feeling it. One day she tried to fix me up with a poor, unsuspecting door-to-door pots and pans salesman. I still insisted that I was not interested in marriage or children, but to Augusta this was just some poor self-image denial crap. A life without marriage and children was unfathomable to her. Luke we did not talk about.

With four babies, well three newborns and one toddler, Sundays were one long baby fest. I did love all my nephews and my niece and clamored to hold them just like all my sisters and my mom did. They never touched the floor when they were at Grandma's. As soon as one person looked ready to set a child down, a new set of arms appeared to whisk the child away.

It was the summer of the above ground pool. Everyone decided we would finally get a swimming pool so Hobart picked up a kit for an 8-foot diameter pool. An 8-foot circle had be cleared, although a spot was chosen that took advantage of whatever grassless spots were left. All stones had to be cleared from the space and sand laid down and raked out level. Then the plastic retaining wall could be put together, the liner smoothed into place, and the caps that held the liner could be snapped over the liner. The filter was assembled and placed but would not be turned on until the pool was full. This project was much easier than the cellar wall project and was actually completed in one Sunday. The guys, Dean, Tyler, Jason and Robert got quite drunk on beer. Hobart was grouchy and disapproving. By the end of the day the hose was in the pool, the babies were cranky and Hobart was somewhat mollified with a good barbecue.

Sundays that summer were spent in the pool and the backyard, although the moms, Felicity, Gertie, and Sara, spent most of their time watching babies and helping with lunch and dinner. The guys spent most of their time working on cars, standing around with beers, belching, farting, getting hot and sweaty, and finally jumping in the pool. Sometimes they got a little too fried and threw women in the pool who were not even dressed for swimming. Hobart knew his sons liked their beers, but he never realized how much until drinking was not intermixed with work, but instead with recreation and hijinks. It was obvious that Hobart regretted putting up that pool.

The Taylors started to have arguments about child rearing. After all there were three new adults in the family who had not been raised in the Taylor household. Dean had spent a lot of time at our house as a teenager and he also grew up in Smithvale, but his mom was a stern no-nonsense kind of woman. He did not have a brother, just three sisters. Felicity and Dean did not always see eye-to-eye where Abby was concerned, Felicity coming down on the side of being at the baby's beck and call, Dean on the side of letting the child cry sometimes. The Taylors were not sympathetic to Dean.

Sara was just a plain fuss-budget, perfectly reasonable probably considering the boys had almost died, but still miles away from the laid back Taylor style. She had the number for Poison Control memorized, and, if speed dial had been available then, the number would have been programmed in. Gertie's Jason was from a very dysfunctional family and he was a Southern boy. He still talked about rebels and Yankees and nothing Gertie did with his son satisfied him. (He did think of the baby as "his".) The Taylor clan absorbed the newcomers, but was altered by them. There is nothing like a big, friendly family, though, and we changed them too.

Robert was also showing signs of settling down. One of Morgan's friends was hanging around and Robert was not pushing this Ellen girl away. He was embarrassed about it, God forbid anyone should tease him (Mr. Torture), but when they thought they could avoid notice by the big mouths (Tyler, Dean and Jason) they say side-by-side on the couch, not saying much, but obviously intent on proximity.

My life had nothing in common with my brothers and sisters lives. They had no idea how my life went from day to day and I'm sure they did not want to know. I liked my life but I knew better than to share too many of the details. Obviously, they knew Annie and had met Linda. They knew about Lena by reputation, but had never met her, and they knew Luke because he used to hang out with Robert. They knew about my losing my job and about the Austin Healey, but we did not discuss the job search I was supposed to be conducting or how I was paying for the car. I suspected they talked about me a lot when I wasn't around.

When I was home with the Taylors, however, I did as the Taylors did. If I arrived stoned, I left straight, not being a big drinker. I held babies, discussed babies, cooked, set tables, did dishes and swam like everyone else. But I didn't fit in like everyone else and I thought they were the backward ones, the ones who were marching out of tune with the times. And even though I didn't fit in, I kept going home, not wanting to completely surrender my membership in the Taylor clan. And I wouldn't have missed the babies for anything, but I would have been happy to miss Augusta's concern and Hobart's disregard. I was in the 60's, but my family was still in the 50's. And I knew how to inhale.

Chapter 21

In Which I Move Six Times in Six Days

Move #1

I decide to go to Boston. After all I have a degree. I'll try a big, new city. Annie's not happy. It leaves her all alone with Linda and it means they have to look for a roommate. But that isn't what happens because Linda decides to move next door with Peter and so they give up the flat and both move to Peter's flat.

After consolidating my possessions drastically, everything I own fits into the Austin Healey Sprite. I'm too naïve to be nervous. After prolonged good byes (especially to Luke) I hit the road. That evening I'm there. I go to Cambridge. I park. I walk past Harvard Yard and peek in. Beautiful, classic. It's September and the quadrangle is all reds and yellows and ambers and browns, the sidewalks covered with leaves. I ask around and find a boarding house. Nothing beautiful here, strictly utilitarian, but clean. Parking the Austin Healey near the boarding house is a hassle, but I persevere and finally locate a space. The owner of the boarding house hires me to clean rooms in exchange for my room rent.

Wandering around Cambridge in the fall is not too shabby. Little movie theaters with artsy facades, tons of restaurants, delis, every price from next to nothing to your eyeteeth. I'm living on a credit card and it has to last. If I don't find a real job soon I will even have to take a cash advance to meet my next car payment. I go to several employment agencies. They are not optimistic. Apparently almost every resident of Cambridge who is old enough has a bachelor's degree. Even people's nannies have degrees. There are colleges all over Boston.

I buy the paper and religiously go through it. I dress up every day and go out looking but I'm not feeling so well. I'm tired all the times, I'm nauseous, no fever. I just ignore it and keep cleaning the boarding house and looking, looking, looking for work. I didn't even have any interviews. I never got that far. I could probably have worked in the public schools, at least as a sub, but after my previous experience I had lost my confidence.

Eventually I located a job as a cook for an MIT fraternity on Beacon Street. Beautiful old house. The fraternity had been split in half by the college as punishment for some computer "borrowing" that had taken place the previous year. Although the fraternity usually had forty members, twenty had been banned from the house in a deal to let the house stay open at all. I reasoned that if I could cook for ten Taylors, I could cook for twenty fraternity guys. I'd just double the recipe.

My domain was a big old kitchen in the basement which opened to the frat parking lot, the dumpster, and a view of the Charles River. I never met a faculty advisor. The boys hired me themselves. They gave me a room of my own on the third floor with a panoramic view of the river and the MIT buildings across the river. I could watch my soap operas in the chapter room. I made breakfast, lunch and dinner, but lunches were usually take-away fare.

I knew nothing about the economics of commercial cooking. The guys got the best. Everyday suppliers brought their wares right into my kitchen, the very best cuts of meat, the freshest vegetables, anything frozen my heart desired. Even beverages were delivered. Apparently among professional cooks alcoholism is frequently a problem. The guys were happy to have someone who was sober in the kitchen. We had simple meals, meat, starch, vegetable, bread. We often ate Italian food as that was in my repertoire. They let me adopt a kitten from the dumpster. You could smoke anywhere in the frat house. I was smoking a pack of cigarettes a day.

MIT guys are brilliant. They can deal with anything mechanical or technical. Later I learned they had rigged a camera in the shower. The little pervs. This was the down side of the job. I was a young, attractive, single woman living in a house full of guys. Will was the president of the fraternity, so he was always checking with me to go over my menus and he even helped in the kitchen.

On the first date night at the house I was to cook flank steak, fries, salad, cake. The cakes were done ahead of time. We had twenty flank steaks, one for each couple (a bit excessive you might say). I was keeping fries warm after deep-frying by scooping them into a metal bowl in the oven. Once when the bowl was sitting on the stovetop waiting for its next load of fries I forgot that the bowl was hot and gripped it with my bare hands. I did not feel the heat right away and by the time I screamed and removed my hands, they were badly burned.

Will had to administer first aid, and finish cooking and serving (via a dumb waiter that connected the kitchen to the dining room. We were thrown together a lot. He was from Hawaii, way far from home and very, very sweet. He was a short guy but I was short too. We developed an attraction for each other and eventually I moved into his room. He ferreted out the camera in the shower and made sure it didn't make a reappearance.

Annie came to Boston with her new roommate, Grace. It was wonderful to spend some time with other women and they were really impressed with my kitchen. Knowing Annie she was probably her to meet an MIT guy, but they all proved too geeky for her. We hung around the kitchen, talking and laughing, eating one maraschino cherry for every time we had ever 'done it.' Grace had a live-in boyfriend so she had 'done it' a lot. By the time they left I realized I was homesick, even though I talked to Mom every week.

It was November. Looking out the back door of the kitchen I saw thousands of people on foot, pouring over the Charles River Bridge between MIT and Beacon Street. I knew it was Moratorium Day and they were marching to end the war in Vietnam. The number of marchers stunned me. I also was facing the reality that I was pregnant. With all the nervousness of relocation I had not noticed that my period had failed to arrive for several months now. I counted. It had to have happened just before I left in September. So we had September, October and half of November. I had switched my birth control method because some of those side effects from the pill were showing up. There had been a few lapses with my new method. I hadn't been worried because I was leaving. That part of my life was over. This was my "new" life.

But here I was in a strange city, with all these guys depending on me to be their cook, and with Will, who I really liked, taking such good care of me.

Will invited me to go spend a day on Cape Cod with him. The guys could take care of their own meals for the day. It was an unseasonably warm November day. I would have been excited to be by the ocean with Will, but I knew that I would have to tell him my news. I knew he would probably think the baby was his. Oh no! I have become a story in True Confessions magazine. He did think he was the father but I explained that he couldn't be.

"What will you do?" he said

"Go home," I said.

"I'm so sorry," I said.

"It's OK," he comforted. He held me close.

"What about the cooking," I said.

"We'll hire someone new," he said. "You're making us broke anyway. We spent our food budget for the year in less than three months," he said. "We've already had to ask our parents for more money."

"But who will you get this time of year," I said.

"Probably another alcoholic," he said.

He hired the new cook quickly and helped me pack up the Austin Healey, which had a new dent from a Boston driver who pulled out of a parking space into the side of my car because he couldn't see it. It was sad to say good-bye but Will said they had appreciated having good food for at least three months of the year. He said if I needed him I should call. I wanted him to finish school. I knew I wasn't going to call him. I was really scared about what was ahead. I didn't know what I would do. I certainly didn't plan to involve Luke. He was too young.

Move #2 and #3 (sort of)

Annie got Peter to agree that I could stay there until I decided what to do and got back on my feet. I was so in debt from my trip to Boston, still had my car payments, had no savings, and now no job. Peter didn't want me but he had agreed and he stuck to his part of the bargain. I did not feel that I was at all ready to have a child. I could barely take care of myself. I was immature and floundering. Abortion was illegal.

I talked it over with Augusta and Hobart. They took out a loan so I could fly to London and have an abortion. I was filled with dread every day. I had never flown in a plane except once in Wing Scouts when we all saved up and flew to a city one hour away by air and then turned around and flew right back. I had never been to England. I had never thought I would have to go off by myself and get an abortion. But I went. It only took three days. I flew there pregnant and sick and frightened. I flew back three days later lighter, sicker and sadder.

I saw almost nothing of England. I walked on King's Row. I saw the red double-decker buses. I had toast for breakfast in one of those silver toast holders they use, all the toast points pointing up. I saw a doctor on Harley Street. I saw a pharmacy near my hotel. I saw a hospital, clean and neat, with nurses dressed like nuns. I rode in one of those black taxicabs that look like refugees from the 1940's. My cab driver insisted he drive me past Buckingham Palace. I saw Heathrow airport. And that was my trip to London.

I couldn't go home to Peter's. I had spent the night with his downstairs neighbor one night when Peter wanted to have an orgy. The neighbor was married, but his wife was away for the weekend. Now I was officially a slut. I had never imagined myself growing up to be a slut.

Move #4

When I got back Linda and Lena were "in love", which I guess had been going on for some time and had decided to live together. Neither of them worked. They were drug dealers. I moved into a rented room in the Appleby Street area. They moved into an apartment right across the street. This area was adjacent to the immediate university neighborhood. It was close enough to be full of students.

Everyone called this area the Appleby Nation because all the hippie freaks lived here and there was a communal spirit building. There was a grocery store, a small theater, several restaurants, a five and dime (the last one in the city), some "head shops," and some shops selling the work of local artists. I was sick and just wanted to hide out and lick my wounds. I didn't even have a phone.

Will took a bus from Boston after talking to Annie. He came to see me. I sent him right back to Boston. I let a man pick me up one day and brought him home to my room. He turned out to be a scary lunatic and would not let me leave. Finally I told him my parents expected me to call them and would worry if I didn't. He let me go to the phone booth downstairs. I called Linda and Lena. Lena came over and rescued me. That guy didn't know what hit him. I felt as low as I could get. Apparently I had not yet reached rock bottom.

Move #5

Lena and Linda moved away from Appleby Street. As dealers they couldn't stay in one place too long. They said the police were after them, but at that time I think it was other drug dealers who were after them. They had unwittingly encroached on someone else's turf. They had been dealing only pot. Now they also had a baggy full of all types of capsules and pills. They had black beauty time spansules and crystal meth and methamphetamines. They had LSD.

They sublet their apartment to Luke and his friend "the Weasel" (Alex). Luke and Alex invited me to move in with them. I did and continued my reign of sluttiness, sleeping with both of them. In February, through one of Linda's old friends Howard Cunningham, I got a job as a reading tutor in a college preparatory program. The job was part time and all we did was hook people up to speed reading machines that helped them read faster. Howard was convinced that speed would solve all their reading problems. He said they couldn't comprehend because they were processing information too slowly. I thought this was really bogus, however I was so happy to be back in a classroom, I just went with the flow.

It was an exciting place because it was a "minority" program and the faculty was very diverse, very "hip," and very committed to social change. Everyone, men and women wore jeans, the more worn the better. There were gorgeous, educated, hunky black men with big Afros on the faculty who could turn their "blackness" on and off. Every staff meeting was like theater.

Move #6

In the summer months there was no school and since I was an hourly employee I wasn't getting paid. I got a job as a secretary for a plumbing supply company. I had to put together job quotes, which was a lot like doing college papers. Now that the lease was up on Linda and Lena's apartment the guys were no longer welcome there. According to the landlord there had been complaints about loud music and noise. Hippies do not always make good neighbors, especially if the people nearby are straight. Annie was also at loose ends as Peter was leaving his apartment to get married. Annie and I found an apartment further east on Appleby Street with three floors. The kitchen was in the basement. The living room and bathroom were on the first floor and there was a bedroom on the third floor. The wall next to the stairs was a wall of windows. I was still smoking a pack of cigarettes a day, Marlboros.

Chapter 22
USA, 1970

Movies released in 1970 included: **M.A.S.H., Change of Habit, Tropic of Cancer, Airport, Woodstock, Women in Love, Let It Be, Love Story, The Out-of-Towners, Catch-22, On a Clear Day You Can See Forever, Myra Breckinridge, They Call Me Mr. Tibbs, Sympathy for the Devil, Lovers and Other Strangers, There's a Girl in My Soup, The Owl and The Pussycat.**

On the New York Times Best Sellers Lists that year were: **Deliverance, Papillon, Rich Man, Poor Man, Everything You Wanted to Know About Sex But Were Afraid to Ask, Chariot of the Gods, Islands in the Stream, Love Story, and The Crystal Cave.**

A first class letter cost 6¢ to mail. The average house cost $32,000. CIGARETTES WERE 37¢ A PACK.

On TV we watched the Newlywed Game, The Ed Sullivan Show, The Dating Game, Here's Lucy, Lassie, Ironside, Hogan's Heroes, Gunsmoke, and The Flip Wilson Show among many others.

In "counter culture" news the problems of Biafra begin to be addressed when civil war ended in Nigeria. Led Zeppelin II is the #1 album as the year begins. The #1 song is Bridge Over Troubled Water by Simon and Garfunkel. The Chicago 8 becomes the Chicago 7 and they are acquitted of some charges, but 5 are found guilty and sentenced. Cassius Clay becomes Muhammed Ali. The #1 R&B song is Call Me by Aretha Franklin.

On May 4th four students are killed at Kent State University in Ohio, an event that shocks the nation. SENATE APPROVES THE BILL TO OUTLAW CIGARETTE ADS ON TV AND RADIO, EFFECTIVE JANUARY 1, 1971. The #1 single is Let It Be by the Beatles. The #1 album is Bridge Over Troubled Water. Student unrest forces closure of 400 universities and colleges in May. Paul

McCartney says he wants to spend more time with his family and that he will no longer record with John Lennon. The first Earth Day is held. University demonstrations continue despite closures. Chubby Checker is arrested in Niagara Falls for possession of hashish, marijuana and drug capsules. The Manson trial opens in June. The #1 album is Woodstock. New York rules that abortion is legal in that state if the doctor and his female patient agree. Caesar Chavez's grape boycott ends, the lettuce boycott begins. The #1 album is Blood, Sweat and Tears 3. The ERA Amendment passes a vote in the House. Tarot cards are very popular. It is announced that draft evasion has increased by a factor of ten over the last five years.

In the fall birth control pills enclose the first warnings of possible side effects. Timothy Leary escapes from prison to live in Algeria. In September Jimi Hendrix dies of barbiturate intoxication. In October Janis Joplin dies of an apparent heroin overdose after completing the album Pearl. The cartoon Doonesbury first appears. The #1 album in early November is Led Zeppelin 3, in late November, Abraxes by Santana. The #1 R&B album is Super Bad by James Brown. The New York Times predicts communal living as a trend. As the year ends Paul McCartney files suit for legal dissolution of the Beatles.

In "mainstream" news Diana Ross leaves the Supremes. The #1 song is I Want You Back by the Jackson 5. The Supreme Court orders complete integration in the South by February 1st. Vietnamese leaders say that POW's are criminals and that their names will not be released. The first Boeing 747 Jumbo Jet flight takes place. Twenty school districts defy the February 1st integration order. Unemployment rises throughout the year. The Nerf ball is introduced. Integration battles heat up in March. We are still in Vietnam and the fighting escalates. A Gallup poll reveals that 86% of Americans are against busing to achieve racial balance. An emergency occurs on Apollo 13 concerning oxygen supplies and power. Astronauts are able to finish the mission, but it is a very tense situation. The US invades Cambodia temporarily in a very unpopular move. We leave before year's end. The SALT talks (Strategic Arms Limitation Talks) reopen. Racial violence in Augusta, Georgia forces the government to call out the National Guard.

Police kill two black students during violence at Jackson State University. The IOC bans South African athletes from future Olympic Games until apartheid ends. Eighteen to twenty-one year olds win the right to vote. A picture phone is developed by Bell. High pollution levels are announced on the East Coast. The #1 single is (They Long to Be) Close to you by the Carpenters. Platform shoes are in style for both men and women. The midi length is introduced. The U S provides weapons and troops to Cambodia. The first no-fault insurance law passes in Massachusetts. An extreme Arab commando group hijacks three America-bound aircraft over Europe.

In the fall the South complies with integration laws. NASA cuts the space program. Vietnam vets demonstrate against the war. The Partridge Family, The Odd Couple, and The Mary Tyler Moore Show premiere on TV. The Phil Donohue Show goes national. 40,000 more troops withdraw from Vietnam. A cyclone strikes the coastal island of Bangladesh killing 20,000. Fondue is in. One million cans of tuna are recalled due to high mercury levels.

Chapter 23
The Taylors

I still see my Taylor clan although not every Sunday. Mom may cry over this abortion but she doesn't share it with me. I cry over the abortion but I don't want to share it with anyone. In 1970 New York State makes abortion legal. Maybe it was better to go to London. It's not a place I see every day, but it cost so much money, money my family doesn't have. I feel guilty about the money but I can't pay it back right now. Mom and Dad did not tell my sisters and brothers about the abortion. Even so I know I am a constant topic of conversation, outrage and worry.

Obviously I did not feel very welcome at home right now. I would go home for weddings. It seemed as if everyone was getting married. I put on dresses to go to weddings and tried to look normal. I had a shag hair cut at the time so my hair was not all freaked out. There are pictures of all those weddings in the family albums. In every picture I have a cigarette in my hand. My outfits were nothing like everyone else's I definitely stood out, not necessarily in a good way.

My language has disintegrated a lot. My conversation consists of "far out, "out a'sight", far fucking out," groovy," "can you dig it", "what a hassle," and "fan-fucking-tastic." For this I went to college. I could not talk about my life to these wedding guests. They wouldn't understand. I could not talk about the war in Vietnam, Black Power, integration, White guilt (Afro-American and Native American), the military-industrial complex, or the environment. I could talk about women's liberation because the guys loved to make fun of that. I couldn't talk about "the revolution", which I saw as peaceful but profound. I did not think America would ever be the same. No one wanted to talk about these things at weddings. They wanted to be light-hearted and gossip and play. I didn't want to talk about anything else. I was a bummer. Of course, I couldn't talk about these things "at home" either because no one wanted to, but we had music and marijuana. I didn't need to talk about their lives, I thought. They were living lives we were brought up to live, predictable, boring and hopelessly middle class. At least I had a job to talk about when everyone asked, "What are you doing these days?" I certainly couldn't say sleeping with two guys and staying stoned as often as possible.

Robert got engaged to Ellen that summer. She is Catholic; he is not. He doesn't switch for her but he agrees to raise the children as Catholics. They will have a wedding at St. Bridget's in Smithvale. His friends tease him unmercifully but he pays them no mind. He's shy about being the center of attention but his sense of humor is intact. She will definitely be the leader in the marriage, drinking will always be a problem, but he will always hold a good job and will be a surprisingly responsible dad, considering how he tortured everyone in his younger years.

Felicity is pregnant with her second child. She is a great mom. Abby is happy and always dressed to the nines. Dean is all cleaned up, all 'hoodiness' gone and very presentable. She keeps her house like she keeps her family. She was right. She is good at this and she's happy. Abby is learning to talk, one of the most delightful stages toddlers go through, and we are all endlessly entertained by her.

Tyler has a job repossessing cars. It's dangerous and Sara, although supportive, is not overjoyed about it. He is offered a job with a local corporation, a safer managerial job. He will stay with this job until he retires. They will be moved around all over the eastern United States. Their twins, Brendan and Sean, are never 'toddler talkers'. They go right to full sentences, although for a while they invent their own language, which only Sara can understand. Tyler, Sara and the boys have been living in a small village forty minutes north of Smithvale. They bought an old house, gutted it, and are now rebuilding it. With two toddlers and one very nervous mom, I'm not sure how Sara keeps her sanity. They will have to leave the house unfinished to go off to Chicago and someone else will inherit all their hard work. Tyler and Sara are a team with a vision for the future.

Gertie is also pregnant again. Timmy is smiley and chubby as ever.

He is also a dream child. Sunny and social and smart, I have never seen him in a temper. Jason brags that Timmy reads **Playboy**. What kind of father shows a toddler **Playboy**? His smarmy tastes don't take hold, though I'm beginning to have my doubts about Jason as a husband and father. But Gertie is happy. She's a social girl and they have lots of friends.

Rebecca, Emily, and Morgan are all in high school. They enjoy their expanded family. Rebecca is a drum majorette and her friends have a band. Emily is quieter. Her best friends are her sisters. Morgan is the baby. She's cute and drastically overprotected, but she's feisty too. She has developed an unhealthy passion for Jason's troubled younger brother. With all the supervision she gets she's not in any real danger of derailing.

I am the 'problem child' in my family, which I never thought I would be. Everyone was very protective of my parents and my treatment of them was the main topic of conversation. I did not feel like I was deliberately rebelling or that it was my intent to hurt my parents on purpose. But I was arrogant. "Come the revolution" I would have the inside track on the new American lifestyle.

Chapter 24

Rock and Roll, Summer, 1970

Once Annie and I move into Appleby Street I get ready to settle
down and stop all the moving. I still have the job at the plumbing
supply. Annie still has her retail job. I have to give the Austin Healey
Sprite back to the dealership. They repossess it. I am in bankruptcy.
Every day I catch a bus to work. We furnish our apartment with next
to nothing - two twin beds and a mattress, a beanbag chair and a
stereo. Some album posters on the wall.

Everyday when I arrive home on the bus "the guys" are standing on
our front porch waving to me. Luke and Alex, their tall skinny friend,
Eddie, and their short, stocky friend, Ralph. Once inside we pipe up
the music. Music is of prime importance on Appleby Street. These
are the albums we have:

- The Young Rascals, 1966
- Cream, Disreali Gears, 1967
- Rolling Stone albums: Beggar's Banquet, 1968, Their Satanic
Majesties Request, 1968, Let It Bleed, 1969
- The Beatles: Rubber Soul, 1965, Revolver, 1966, Sgt. Pepper's
Lonely Hearts Club Band, 1967, White Album, 1968, Magical
Mystery Tour, 1968, Abbey Road, 1969, Let It Be, 1970.
- Steve Miller Band, Sailor, 1968, #5, 1970
- Jefferson Airplane: Surrealistic Pillow, 1967, Volunteers, 1969
- The Doors: The Doors, 1967, Waiting for the Sun, 1968, Strange
Days, 1968, Soft Parade, 1969
- Jimi Hendrix: Axis, Bold as Love, 1967, Are You Experienced, 1968
- Bob Dylan: The Freewheelin' Bob Dylan, 1963 Bob Dylan's
Greatest Hits, 1967, John Wesley Harding, 1967, Nashville Skyline,
1969
- Janis Joplin, Big Brother and the Holding Company, 1968
- Creadance Clearwater Rival: Bayou Country, 1968, Green River,
1969
- King Crimson, In the Court of the Crimson King, 1969
- Blood, Sweat, and Tears, Blood, Sweat and Tears, 1969

• Led Zeppelin: Debut Album, 1968, Led Zeppelin II, 1969
• Grand Funk Railroad, Closer to Home, 1970
• Chicago, Chicago Transit Authority, 1969
• Crosby, Stills and Nash, Crosby, Stills and Nash, 1969
• Neil Young: Everybody Knows This is Nowhere, 1969, After the Gold Rush, 1970
• Crosby, Stills, Nash and Young, Déjà Vu, 1970
• Joe Cocker: I Get By with a Little Help From My Friends, 1969
• Pink Floyd, Ummagumma, 1968
• Blind Faith, Blind Faith, 1969
• Santana, Santana, 1969
• Neil Diamond: Touching Me, Touching You, 1969, Taproot Manuscript, 1970
• Simon and Garfunkel: Bookends, 1968, Sounds of Silence, 1968, Bridge Over Troubled Water, 1970
• Steppenwolf, Steppenwolf, 1968
• Van Morrison, Moondance, 1970
• Judy Collins, Who Knows Where the Time Goes, 1968
• James Taylor, Sweet Baby James, 1970
• John Denver, Rhymes and Reasons, 1969
• Mother Earth, Living with the Animals, 1968
• Roberta Flack, First Take, 1969, Chapter Two, 1970
• Laura Nyro, New York Tendaberry, 1969
• Moody Blues: Days of Future Passed, 1968, Threshold of a Dream, 1969

When the boys are there we crank up things like the Rolling Stones, or King Crimson or Steppenwolf or Jimi Hendrix, loud outrageous music with long psychedelic solos in the middle – Pink Floyd, Led Zeppelin, Grand Funk. We get stoned and enjoy the tunes, so complex, engaging our senses, and filled with excitement.

When I am by myself I opt for songs with great lyrics: Bob Dylan, Simon and Garfunkel, Judy Collins, Van Morrison, Neil Diamond. Or I go for straight out romance like James Taylor or Roberta Flack. I like to sing along. The Beatles can go in either group. Janis Joplin is my music too, because the guys are not into her.

On weekends Annie and I go to a small club at the university. They have name bands, although not any of the big time groups from our albums. We go late since Annie has to work weekends. She's still looking for the perfect college educated man. The club is smoky and dark; I can smoke cigarettes there all night long if I want. Annie doesn't meet anyone special, but she does decide that she wants to go to college in the fall. I think it's a great idea for her, but not necessarily for me.

I don't know how our neighbors put up with our music. They never complain though, at least not to us. Annie doesn't care about most of this music, however she is rarely home in the evening and she has the apartment to herself on her days off. When she is off and I am home she spends her hours with the boys and me.

Chapter 25
Summer, 1970, Drugs

Lena and Linda are on the run. They are camping out in state parks because the "pigs" are after them. But we see a lot of them, the boys and me. They stop by in the evening and listen to music with the rest of us. They seem to get along pretty well, which surprises me. Lena is the "butch" and Linda is the "fem." Linda never seemed like the type to bow to authority and Lena is definitely in charge. Still, somehow they get along.

They are always offering everyone in the apartment free drugs. They provide all the grass. The boys drop acid every day and everyone is always saying things like "don't bring me down (usually to me) or "I'm flyin" or "I'm peaking" or "I'm crashing." They don't really act like they're high. They just do the same things we all do. It's summer so we go outside a lot. We go to the park and lay on the hill in the sun. We go to the water tower in the park and watch stars and other people. We sit at concerts in the park and it just seems like an ordinary summer day.

There's an old amphitheater in the park. There is a stage at the bottom of a bowl shaped arena. The seats are built into the grassy slope as terraces. Rocks face each terrace and grass tops it. The amphitheater is invisible from the outside. Trees and an old wrought iron fence surround it. I never knew it was there until this summer. Now the gates are opened up and there are concerts there, and plays and festivals. They are all free. Whole little hippie families show up and sit around on blankets on the grass at the bottom of the bowl. The kids run nearly naked, long hair flying in the wind. Vendors sell jewelry and kites and imported tchothkes. Lots of smoking is going on, both legal and not.

I have never tried acid. In fact I have never tried any drugs except grass and hashish. These drugs sometimes make me high, but sometimes make me paranoid and sleepy. Lena thinks I should branch out. One day I try a black beauty. It doesn't do a thing for me. Another day I try a half a barrel of sunshine acid. Whoa! That does something. The air around me seems thick and syrupy and the light appears layered, like looking through a piece of old, thick glass. My skin tingles, colors fragment, movements blur. When I wave my hands in the air I see afterimages. I'm not sure I like it. It makes my brain feel like it will explode, like I will go crazy and end up hospitalized mewling like a kitten until I'm old and gray. After a while I want my trip to end, but it doesn't go away until the drug leaves your system, almost eight hours. Once in a while if you smoke really strong grass you feel like this, but it wears off quickly. This lasts and lasts. You can't even really sleep through. It certainly is an economical high; you get a lot of bang for your buck. You don't have to keep stopping to refuel. But it's too risky. How do the guys do this every day? Now I know what "trippy" means. I decide that I might give this one more try later, much later. One day someone talks me into trying a "blue dot", which is just a piece of paper with a circular blue splash of chemical something on it. That's milder, my head's in a better place. I have a good trip. Still – not my drug of choice. I decide I will not drop acid again.

I'm tired. We've been partying a little too hearty. There has been a lot of beer and grass over the weekend. I have to get up and go to work but I'm dragging. Lena hands me a little yellow pill. "What's this," I say. "It's methedrine," she says. "It will perk you right up." It does. I have lots of energy now. I also feel smart and confident. I eat my day up and have energy to spare when I get home. This feeling I like. Lena gives me several more. She warns me that although they have these positive effects for a while, they will eventually let you down hard. When you crash, you will feel like shit for a few days.

I like this very efficient, clean feeling I suddenly have so I keep taking the little yellow pills. I start cleaning the apartment feverishly, I don't need food, I can't sit still and when I do I start drawing these very inventive pictures of tiny little mazes on every available sheet of paper. I may be turning into an artist. At work I feel like I'm a whiz.

But eventually I find that my fingertips hurt when I have to type and that my mind cannot stay on one subject, and that I can't look my boss in the eyes while he tries to explain a new project. Lena's gone when I run out of pills. I crash. I miss a day of work. I lose my job. Apparently I wasn't the whiz I thought I was. I still have my tutoring job in September, but right now I'm broke and I'm not happy about it. That's the end of the methedrine. No matter how much I like it, it has to go. I have never been fired from a job before.

It's almost August. Annie got into a state university and she's leaving to go find a place to live in her new college town. The timing couldn't be worse, but she's doing the right thing. Lena and Linda tell me they are tired of camping out. They offer to move in and help with the rent temporarily. They want to stop dealing drugs. They are both thinking about college too. They do have a stockpile though and they need to get rid of that. I tell them they can't live here if they are dealing drugs, but they know I'm a whuss. They plead with me. They say they will hide their stash outside the apartment in the basement and they will not sell out of the apartment. I have no rent money, and worse, I have no cigarettes. I relent and let them stay. They take the bedroom upstairs and I move to the mattress in the living room.

I decide to try another tab of sunshine. Maybe if I try one out in the country, in a beautiful natural setting, it will set me free. I hitchhike to a camp my family members have bought out in the back of beyond. I decide hitchhiking is not for me. Everyone who picks me up is a married man and everyone makes suggestions I am not interested in. I'm lucky, they don't push it. They just let me out of the car. It takes six rides to get where I'm going. I let myself into this flyblown shack, which is my family's, camp and try to make it pretty so I'll see nice things when I'm tripping. I find a good radio station. I don't really know why I'm doing this, to prove something to myself, I think.

I make myself a sandwich with the groceries I brought with me. I eat it standing, looking out the window across the long narrow lawn. There are no other camps around. A green lush wilderness lies beyond the lawn, a dirt road heading straight as an arrow through it. I drink some iced tea from a thermos. I go outside and set up one of those woven plastic chaise lounges that can be laid flat or adjusted for sitting. I put on my bathing suit, drop the tab of acid, and go out to the lounger.

Whoosh! The acid hits and I'm tripping. I don't like it any better this time. The sun is good, it's really pretty out here, but I feel sick to my stomach. I get up and go inside and turn the music up. I'm OK. I somehow get hung up on a mirror. I'm seeing my face as if for the first time. I see my mother there, I see my father. I see my heredity written across my features, my bone structure. I don't really like my face right now. I turn the mirror away. I use the outhouse and think about the past when everyone had one of these odorous contraptions. I think about how convenient our lives are. I am now shivering. I can't stop. I'm not cold; I'm just overwhelmed with drugginess. I change back into my clothes.

The sun is setting. I watch it and shiver. It's beautiful, but I'm feeling sorry for myself. I'm so alone. I forget that that was the whole idea. Lena and Linda are coming to pick me up. It keeps me together. It's dark now. I look out the window. I'm in an alien, wild place. I'm not a nature girl I guess. There are dwarves holding lanterns walking through the tall grass. Look at that! So many of them. I hear the car in the driveway. I can't wait to get out of here. I turn everything off, grab my backpack and as I walk out the door, I realize that there are no dwarves. They are fireflies. I sleep all the way home and vow once again to never take acid. This time I stick to my vow.

Not working is not good for me. I don't feel grounded. I'm nervous and I don't know how to fill up my day. I can't buy cigarettes regularly and I hate when I don't have any. I actually pick up a long butt off the street one day. I think about who might have had it in their mouth before me, but I still fell calmer as soon as I have a couple of puffs. I'm a derelict. I tell myself that in one month I will be working again so I should just try to enjoy my freedom. I try to get a schedule going, have meals at regular times, do the dishes and housework in the mornings and evenings. Read, if I happen to be alone in the afternoons. Lena and Linda don't stay home much, but the boys are here a lot once they actually wake up and start their days.

Lena and Luke's older brother, Lincoln, is at our apartment. He's visiting from the west coast. He's very handsome, blond and muscular. A man, really. I don't know what he's doing here. Why didn't he go to his mom's? Why don't they all visit there? But he sits on a chair in my kitchen. I give him a cup of tea. We don't have much to say to each other but Lena is happy and keeps the conversation humming along. Now I know why he's here instead of home. There's a packet of cocaine sitting on my kitchen table. He wants to share it with all of us. I don't really want to try it. This is a serious drug. One you can get hooked on. I once met this couple who were jazz musicians. They were also heroin addicts. Every time they went into a methadone program, one would drop out and go back to heroin. Then the other one would join them. Back and forth they went. They were very much in love, terribly co-dependent, and totally miserable.

But I was curious and saying no did not seem worth the hassle. Link got out a mirror, spilled some coke on it and cut it into lines. He rolled a five-dollar bill into a tight straw and we each, in turn, snorted a line. Coke is also called ice because of the way it makes you feel. It reminded me of methedrine.

Thank goodness I did not want to do it again. I decided I was through with all drugs except, once in a while, pot. No more pills, no more acid, no more anything. I really liked my natural state the best. I was saved from a drug addiction, but I'm not sure how. It may have been just a matter of body chemistry. But I was still going along with my deal to let Lena and Linda sell the rest of their LSD.

Chapter 26
Summer, 1970, Sex

Sex was a pretty scarce commodity on Appleby Street that summer. Someone may have been having sex, but it wasn't me. Annie had a perm in her long, brown hair and it looked really good. Just a little too good. The guys took to calling her "jungle woman." Luke became "forest man." I was jealous. There was some chemistry between them. One day they really got into their roles and started jumping up on the ledges along the stairwell and pretending to whip each other. There was definitely some sexual energy there. But if they ever consummate their lust it is not when I am around. And I don't want to know.

Of course Lena and Linda probably "do it" after they move in. They're upstairs – I don't have to see it. I don't know and I don't want to know. Downstairs they're affectionate, but not mushy. Besides Lena is not someone who sits around. They are usually up and out.

Luke and I have one very hot afternoon when he takes his slow time and makes every inch of me feel closely and intimately loved. We finish at the same moment and he holds me and says he will always love me. We love each other. We are not in love. In fact that is the last time we are together like that. There was someone in the other twin bed. Some female. I don't remember who – well I do but it was not someone we ever saw again. When it was all over, she said, "That was beautiful." So I never really know if I was a surrogate lover, or if it was really real. Still the experience makes an imprint on my mind and body.

The day I take the blue dot acid we all go to a park with a falls. We're the only ones there. It's a gorgeous summer day. Brown water with gray rocks and white foam, scattering sunlight. The cheerful water trickling over the shale shelves of rock behind and splashing into the pool beneath. Somehow Annie and I end up stripping to our panties to play in the water. I'm sure the guys enthusiastically encourage us. We are usually pretty modest in spite of our hippie lifestyle, but we feel liberated and naughty. After we cavort for a while we sit on a blanket in the sun to dry. We have no towels. Our clothes are not nearby. Some other people arrive at the park, two young urbanite couples, very straight, no children. They invite themselves to sit down with us on the blanket. They ask questions, try to carry on a conversation. I hate it, the cover of the **Blind Faith** album not-withstanding. I know Annie hates it. We feel really naked now. When we can move we get into our clothes really fast. Thus ends our adventures in nudity.

That is about the extent of the sex I have in this apartment on Appleby Street. Luke and I are finally done with sex. Alex and I have been done for a while. I become more like a mom, making meals, offering cups of tea and coffee, making lemonade, packing picnics to take on various outings, straightening the apartment every day. I make beds, clean the bathroom, wash and dry the dishes. I actually find these routine chores soothing. I put on music, loud. I sing while I work and dance with my arms waving over my head. I think, what if I went through all of this just to give myself permission to be ordinary?

Chapter 27

Summer, 1970, Cigarettes

When I have cigarettes I smoke thirty cigarettes a day. I don't think ahead and hoard cigarettes for when I run out. When I have them, I smoke full out. When I don't I come to a screeching halt. They you don't want to be around me. I get sarcastic and mean, my speech clipped and angry. That's it, I'm angry. I rarely show any anger any other time. Also I feel light-headed and shaky and nervous. I hate being without cigarettes. I don't know what to do with myself. Time stretches; minutes seem like hours. Someone give a cigarette! My friends do try to keep me in cigarettes because they don't really like this me as much as the anesthetized version.

I have a cigarette as soon as I wake up. Still in my nightgown, I turn on the Today Show. I light up another cigarette in the bathroom, put it out while I shower. With my wet hair wrapped in a towel I relight the cigarette and inspect my face in the mirror. I deal with any irregularities there and head downstairs to the kitchen. I don't need to carry the ashtray. I have a new one on each level. I light a new cigarette as I put on the water for instant coffee. I drink it black, a remnant of the vending machine my first year of teaching, the black coffee being the only drinkable choice. I move over to the tiny kitchen table where there is, of course, another ashtray and eat my breakfast, usually just toast. I don't smoke while I eat, but as soon as I am done I light another one. I put my dishes in the sink and head back upstairs, back to the bathroom with my coffee. I smoke 3 cigarettes while I dry and style my hair and another while I put on my very light makeup.

My one splurge has always been Elizabeth Arden moisturizer because my skin likes it best. It's very pricey but I still have some left. I usually ask for it for Christmas which I still spend with Augusta and Hobart, et al. Now I have two Christmases because I have another with my friends. That's the extent of my "toilette" for the day.

I'm still in my nightgown as I head into the living room. I light my

147

next cigarette as spend a few minutes with the Today show, just enough to hear the news of the day. I have a little dresser now in the living room so I paw through the drawers picking out the outfit of the day. Perhaps some baggy shorts and a short-sleeved blouse. I'm already wearing sandals with my nightgown. I light another cigarette before I head back to the bathroom to get dressed. There is a new Vogue in the living room waiting for me. I love Vogue, it's not really like fashion, it's like art. I light a new cigarette and it sits in the ashtray smoking while I turn my bed back into a couch. I spend a long time with Vogue. I don't just look at it; I read it. I smoke three more cigarettes while I do this.

There's no one else home right now so I have the place to myself. I need to go to the store. I need a new pack of cigarettes and we need a few groceries. Lena has left me some money. After I lock the front door, I light a cigarette before I leave the front porch. The grocery store is only a block away, a long block. I mostly hold the lit cigarette down at my side. I don't really like strangers on the street to see me actually puffing it. I think it's really not right to smoke on the street. When there's no one around, I take a puff and blow the smoke out impatiently. Some people like to watch their smoke and play with it. I've done it. There is pleasure in it, but for me the pleasure is pretty much oral. I put the cigarette out before I go in the store. When I come out with my groceries I light up again.

Time for lunch. Repeat of breakfast. Light up, prepare lunch, eat lunch, have an after lunch ciggie. Dishes are added to the pile. If it isn't a laundry day, which involves a trip down the street in the opposite direction from the grocery store, then it's soap opera time. I watch two so that's two hours, about four smokes. The telephone rings. I light up and talk to Mom. She says, "You're smoking aren't you?" She can hear me exhale.

The guys stop by. Lena and Linda come home. I'm still on the couch watching TV. We chat; we commune through the music, the words of it, the complexity of it, the familiarity of it. Our favorite albums right now are King Crimson and Déjà Vu (Crosby Stills, Nash, and Young). "Our House" is our very favorite song. We all sing the words either out loud or in our head, "is a very, very, very fine house." I have five cigarettes while we do this.

Time for dinner. I make macaroni and cheese, there's a veggie, white bread, lemonade, no dessert. I smoke while I set out the plates. We can't eat at the table. We just fill a plate and eat where we want. After dinner I light up again. It's pretty smoky in here by now, because some of the guys smoke too. I collect all the dishes; fill the dishpan with detergent and water. My cigarette is right next to me burning down to ashes, but if I try to smoke it now it will get all wet and disintegrate. If I want a puff I have to dry my hands first. I pile all the dishes into the drainer; cover them with a dishtowel. I let them air dry.

I put on long pants because we have tickets to hear the Moody Blues at the university. I light up one last cigarette before we go in – you can't smoke at this concert. Someone has made hash brownies and is passing them around. There are enough for us so we each eat one. The hash is so strong that the walls of the auditorium change color. Someone else passes around giant cucumbers. It's a double entendre. Everyone gets the joke. "Must have big one." The band comes on and they're wonderful. We all get very mellow.

As soon as I leave the concert I light up, but I have to put it out when I get in the car. We go home, open some beers, light up some jays and sprawl out on my couch-bed. At around 2 am we are finally all crashed or gone home. That is five cigarettes later. Oh, oh, today I went over. I smoked thirty-two. The next day I get up and do it all over again for the next forty years, although I eventually get down to less than one pack a day.

Chapter 28

The Shit Hits the Fan

It's Tuesday, mid-August. I'm home alone. I'm following my usual morning routine. I have no cigarettes so I'm not in a good place. Cleaning and grooming give me no peace today. I'm on autopilot. Finally, it's about 11 am. I hear a knock at the door, then silence. If it was someone I knew they would be yelling, "Zoe, Zoe." No yells. I shrug and continue with the casserole I'm making for dinner, tuna noodle, I know, yuck. It's cheap and it stretches. What can I say?

The knock comes again, louder this time. I head up the stairs to the front door. When I peer out I see a sort of nerdy guy who comes here once in a while to see Lena. He has someone else with him, a very beautiful young woman. Now this is an unlikely pair. I don't want to open the door, but I do. Nerd guy says don't I remember him; his name is Tom. I do remember him, but have never spoken to him, however, I say, "I know who you are."

"This is my cousin," he tells me, "She's moving here from Chicago."

"Poor baby," I say.

I introduce myself. She tells me her name is Rose.

"What can I do for you?" I say.

"We're here to see Lena," Tom says.

"Lena's somewhere babysitting," I say (of all things – but it's true. Lena's practicing. She wants to have a baby she has decided. Her ex will be the father.)

"Do you mind if we wait for her awhile," he says.

"It could be a long wait." I say.

"We'll wait," he says.

Now I have two virtual strangers on my hands. I can't exactly show them into the drawing room and leave them. There is no drawing room. Tom takes the beanbag chair and Rose sits on the couch-bed.

"Would you like some coffee or tea?" I say, always the hostess. "Coffee," they say together.

I go down to the kitchen, make three cups of coffee and carry them back up. My brain is buzzing from lack of nicotine. Now I'm going to add caffeine to the mix. I need to run around the block. But I can't, there are two people in my living room.

"How could you stand to leave Chicago?" I say.

"I came to help out my aunt," she says. "But I do need to find a job."

"What do you do?" I ask.

"I'm a dancer," she tells me.

Oh my god, a dancer, in my living room. I love dance – ballet, tap, jazz. I don't care. I wish I was a dancer, I think.

"What kind of dance?" I ask her.

"Go-go," she replies. "I'm not an exotic dancer," she warns, "Strictly cage dancing."
"I don't think we have any go-go clubs here," I say.

I spy the morning paper. I pull out the classifieds and hand them to her. I find a pen.

"Look in here," I say.

I know there are no go-go jobs in our newspaper. After all, I've been to just about every club in the city with Annie. I just don't feel right about these two. It's making me nervous. I'm already on edge from coffee and no cigarettes. When I'm with strangers and on edge, I talk a blue streak to cover my nerves and any uncomfortable silences. This is not a good thing.

"Maybe you could sell a local club on the idea?" I babble. "There must be other dancers here who would love a job like that."

I describe several clubs to her that I think would be appropriate. She dutifully writes them down on some notepaper I give her. Hey, we have time I think.

"Let me look up the numbers for you," I say, grabbing the phone book. I'm a job counselor.

"That's not necessary," she says, but she writes down the numbers.

I'm so antsy by now there are free radicals or bouncy ions or something flying all over the room. I want them out of here. I clear the cups away to the kitchen just to have a breather. When I come back Rose says that they think they will go. They'll see Lena some other time. Tom stays behind after he sends Rose out onto the porch.

"Give me a minute," he says.

"Now what," I think.

Turns out he's having an acid emergency. He wants to buy five tabs of acid. This has nothing to do with me. I don't own any acid. The stuff belongs to Lena and Linda. But he won't go away. Rose keeps sticking her head in the door saying, "Is everything OK, and Tom keeps waving her off.

Finally, I reason that if I sell him one tab of acid then maybe they'll go away and maybe I can buy a pack of cigarettes. I tell him to go wait on the porch with Rose. I call Lena and tell her who's here and what he wants. She says to go ahead and give it to him. He's a regular customer. I ask if I can use a little of the money to buy cigarettes.

She says, "abso-fuckin-lutely."

"Thanks, Lena," I say, "See you later."

How gullible am I, how naïve, how stupid? To any normal person this would smell like a set-up. But these are my friends. My instincts are trying to tell me no, don't touch this. But my cigarette addiction and my too-many-fiction-heroes brain are canceling out the no. I put my head out the door and beckon Tom over.

"I can only sell you one," I say.

"How much?" he asks.

"Two dollars," I say.

I don't know what Lena charges but this seems like a fair price to me. And it will cover a pack of cigarettes with some left over for Lena.

"Wait out on the porch," I tell him.

I go into the basement. I retrieve one tab of acid from the baggie over the furnace. I go back upstairs and beckon Tom back into the house. I take the two dollars and hand over the tab of sunshine. They finally leave.

I feel weird about the whole encounter but once I am alone, and once I have my cigarettes, I try to put it out of my mind. I have known for a while that not all "hippie freaks" are about peace, love and changing the world. Some just want to get high. Some are just there to rip off people who are high. But I think my friends are loyal to our small "family" group. I don't even stop to think that some of my behavior with Luke may not have struck a positive chord with his sister. I've never asked Luke, but I don't think I've actually wounded him. I could be wrong though.

Chapter 29

Busted

I was looking out the window when the police cars pulled up. There were two. They pulled up fast, lights flashing. I can't for the life of me remember what color they were. Three policemen and one policewoman came across the front yard running. I was really scared. I was home alone. I wanted to run downstairs through the kitchen and out the basement door, but there wasn't time.

I opened the door at their very authoritative rap and stepped back as they swooped into the living room. Our living room was small. You could see it all in one glance. There was very little in the way of furniture. A stereo system took up one wall under the window with all the albums filed neatly into crates except the few I had been playing. On the opposite wall was a mattress on the floor with a quilted cover and piles of pillows. There was an American flag forming a canopy on the ceiling in front of the fireplace at the end of the room opposite the door. This flag enraged the police who showed how they felt with looks and eyebrows rather than words. They did not pull it down completely only pulling one corner away from the ceiling letting the flag flop down, but not letting it touch the floor. Nothing fell out when they loosened the flag so the search went on.

I tried to stay out of their way and the one policewoman hung around me to make sure I did. Across from the fireplace was a three-story wall of windows with no curtains. A stairway went down along the wall of windows and another stairway went up. The bathroom was on the same floor as the living room and was quickly dealt with but I couldn't see where they looked and I knew there was nothing there.

Downstairs was the kitchen, a tiny dining ell and the door to the basement. Up the other flight of stairs was the bedroom. I don't remember them searching the bedroom. I think the whole search was just an act. Someone had told them right where the stuff was. But they made a good show of it. They got into the cupboard and looked through the flour and sugar scattering flour everywhere, all over my clean dishes sitting in the dish drainer, all over my clean floor.

Oh, I was plenty scared. I was shaking uncontrollably. I never pictured such a thing happening in my life. It was quite surreal.

And then they went out into the basement, behind the furnace and found the baggie full of tabs of sunshine acid, the yellow barrel type, the good stuff. I wasn't sure they could prove it was ours being that it was outside our apartment in the shared basement, but thinking it over later, I was sure someone had squealed, had informed and told them where the hiding place was because, after the little 'search show', they went right to it. Much later, it dawned on me that hardly anyone knew the hiding place.

At the time, though, I was way too busy being scared. I had on a little sun dress which was pretty bare and what with my nerves and my shivering I was covered in goose bumps even though I was hugging myself tightly. When it became clear that I was going in the squad car to jail, I asked the police woman if I could change into something warmer and less revealing. The men did not want to wait but she let me. I hadn't given them any trouble and I was polite. To tell the truth, I was in shock.

After I changed my dress for jeans and a blouse, they took me out the front door. I was wearing handcuffs. My shock deepened. They cuffed me in front of my body, not behind my back and led me across our front lawn to the car where they did that head thing while they put me in the back seat. I'm sure I cried.

They drove downtown and parked behind the Public Safety Building, a parking lot I had never seen before. They took me into the jail, into a land where you could not enter or leave any space without waiting for someone to unlock a really serious set of bars. The doors clanged open and shut.

I was fingerprinted, photographed and strip searched, but sent to a cell in my own clothing. Yes I wanted a cigarette, I wanted about ten cigarettes, but I wasn't allowed any, nor did I have any. I didn't ask for a phone call. I didn't want anyone to know. Maybe the system could just swallow me up. Augusta and Hobart, I did not want them to know, not my cute little innocent parents who did not belong anywhere near this place.

I was in a cell by myself, right next door to a heroin addict who was in withdrawal and very sick. She kept puking and moaning, asking that someone do something. Finally they switched our cells so she would be closer to the guards and I got the pukey cell. Luckily most of the puking must have been dry heaves.

In the morning I was faced with my two little sweet parents walking down the hall towards me and the courtroom for the arraignment. I had been on TV. Everyone saw me. The entire Taylor clan was traumatized. Smithvale was traumatized. But I was the most traumatized of all. Life can change in a minute and mine just did.

Epilogue

Felicity has her second baby, a girl. She gets to enjoy her girls until they are one-and-a-half and three. On a snowy day in 1973 she drives into the back of a parked truck and dies. She has her seat belt on but she still dies. She had everything she always wanted but she loses it. How is this fair? As soon as he can function, Dean raises the girls himself. He does this for eight years. Then he marries a divorced hairdresser with two boys of her own. She becomes like another sister and we don't lose Felicity's kids.

Tyler and Sara are still being moved all over the eastern U.S. They move to New Jersey when the boys are in high school. When they have to leave New Jersey the twins stay behind. They earn degrees at Rutgers and get married to New Jersey girls. Their weddings are one month apart. They each have three children, two boys and a girl. Tyler has the most financial success of anyone in the family.

Gertie and Jason have two boys. After fourteen years of marriage Jason has an affair so blatant that Gertie cannot ignore it. She has to leave him. Jason turns mean. Gertie has a really bad five years and then she remarries. Both her sons marry. One has two girls. The other has one child out of wedlock, he marries a woman with two girls and then they have twin girls.

Robert marries Ellen. They also have to travel around. He is in the shoe business. They have a son and twin daughters, who are beautiful, but bald for the first two years of their lives. Their son is married and has three children, two boys and one girl. One of the twins is married, she has three children.

Emily marries twice. Both marriages end badly. She lives in the South for quite a while. Rebecca lives with her for a while. She has two daughters by her second husband. She's an accountant. She eventually moves back to Smithvale. One of her daughters is married with three children. Her older daughter also marries and has two children.

Rebecca never marries but she is the family link. Everyone in the family likes her and relies on her. She lives with Augusta who is 99 and doing fine. Hobart died of prostate cancer at 81. She has 13 grandchildren and 17 great grandchildren so far. Rebecca is also the family historian and a computer whiz.

Morgan marries a guy who fixes jets. She is a mail carrier. They live by a river and have two daughters. Morgan keeps her feistiness and her sense of humor. We hold all our family parties at her house.

Annie is my friend for forty years. She finally met the man of her dreams and after a lengthy courtship they marry. They have two children, a son and a daughter. I am privileged to watch them grow up over summers when they visit from Florida. Annie teaches elementary school.

Me, Zoe, I am lucky and unlucky. One month after my first arrest by the city police, the county police come to my school to arrest me again. The school secretary warns me. I turn myself in and only have to stay three hours. I don't get fired. Thank goodness it's an "alternative" school. After two court-appointed lawyers and after I call the DA a hypocrite (I do know how to sabotage myself), I am convicted through a plea bargain of a felony for possession of a controlled substance. I am sentenced to two years of probation and two years of psychotherapy. I should have fought harder but I cannot bring myself to borrow any more money from anyone.
The psychotherapy is good. I obviously need it. I teach at the same school for 23 more years. I become an assistant professor, and a department chair. I get a master's degree. I feel I do a good job as a teacher. I get to send hundreds of students to college or help them get a GED. When I leave there I can't get another teaching job. Even with a "Relief from Disability" signed by a judge. The climate has changed. Public school parents won't have this and I don't blame them. I take an architecture course and they tell me that a felony conviction will prevent me from being a licensed architect. I retire early. I work temp jobs. I'm a cashier. I will be a felon all my life. It's OK. I was perhaps way luckier than I deserved to be.

I have quit smoking three times, but as I write these words I continue to puff away. The cosmic roulette wheel doesn't let you get away with these things forever. Finally, after I finish this story I use Chantix and stop smoking. But I was a smoker for 40 years.

Lena and Linda hire a $5000 attorney and are convicted of misdemeanors. I don't see them again.

Luke dies too young, although not as young as Felicity. I don't know about it until after the fact. Augusta knows, but she doesn't tell me. A mutual friend tells me that he died of a drug overdose. I hope that's not true.

Back in the day…

N. L Brisson writes for her own website **The Armchair Observer**. She has a BA degree from SUNY Potsdam and a Master of Education from the University of Arizona at Tucson. She taught College Reading and Study Skills for 24 years. She lives in central New York, in a place with very snowy winters.

Brisson, N. L.